Cast in Time

Book 2: Baron of the Middle Counties

By Ed Nelson

Other books by Ed Nelson

The Richard Jackson Saga

Book 1: The Beginning

Book 2: Schooldays

Book 3: Hollywood

Book 4: In the Movies

Book 5: Star to Deckhand

Book 6: Surfing Dude

Book 7: Third Time is a Charm

Book 8: Oxford University

Book 9: Cold War

Book 10: Taking Care of Business

Book 11: Interesting Times

Book 12: Escape from Siberia

Book 13: Regicide

Book 14: What's Under, Down Under?

Book 15: The Lunar Kingdom

Book 16: First Steps

Stand Alone Stories

Ever and Always

Mary, Mary

The Cast in Time series

Book 1: Baron

Dedication

This book is dedicated to my wife, Carol, for her support and help as my first reader and editor.

With special thanks to Ole Rotorhead for his technical insights on how things really work.

Then there are my beta readers: Ole Rotorhead, Lonelydad, Antti Huotari, and Pat O'Dell.

And never forget the professional editor, Morgan Waddle.

Quotation

According to 'M' theory, ours is not the only universe. Instead, 'M' theory predicts that a great many universes were created out of nothing.

Stephen Hawking

Copyright © 2023

Map of Cast in Time Cornwall

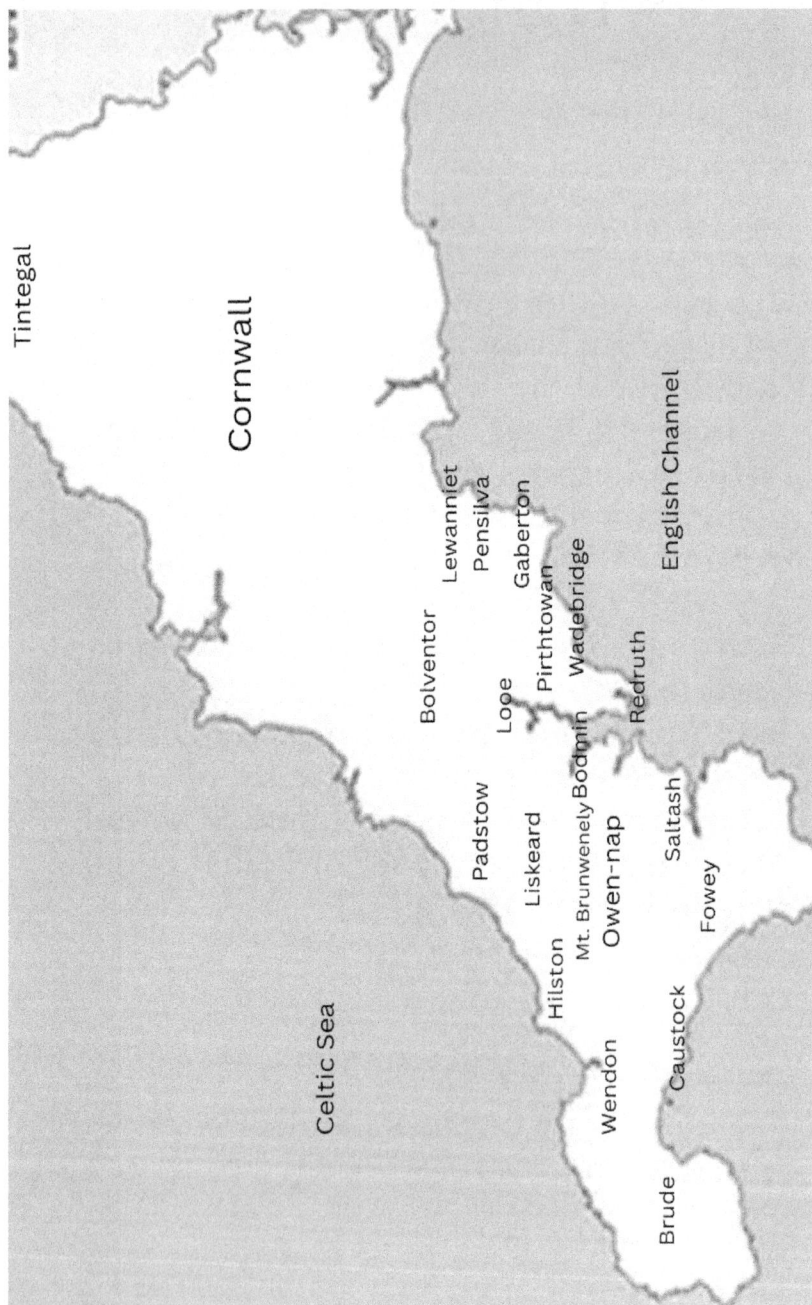

Tintegal

Cornwall

Lewanniet

Pensilva

Gaberton

Pirthtowan

Wadebridge

English Channel

Bolventor

Looe

Redruth

Padstow

Liskeard

Mt. Brunwenely Bodmin

Owen-nap

Saltash

Hilston

Fowey

Celtic Sea

Wendon

Caustock

Brude

Table of Contents

Contents

Chapter 1

Now that I had conquered Pirthtowan and Wadebridge, I had to integrate them into my Barony. I hadn't wanted to go to war with them, but they tried to assassinate me, so I had no choice.

Their failed attempt resulted in the death of the Dowager Countess Wendon and her son, the only male heir to the Barony. I had grown fond of them and had a good relationship with her father, John Chandler.

John, a ship's Chandler in Saltash, was also a friend and business partner. I couldn't leave their deaths unanswered. There was also the fact that once they had tried and failed, they had no choice but to continue.

But they only had to get lucky once. I had to win successfully against every attempt. So I set out with my war party the next morning.

I would like to report that we won a series of hard-fought battles. The fact of the matter was we rolled them up easily. My introduction of a stronger crossbow was the deciding factor.

Thad, my assistant scribe, attended to me as usual. He had accompanied me enough to know what was needed.

It would take weeks to give the locals an understanding of the changes that would be made. Followed by months of work to implement the changes.

The first step was to send the headmen of Pirthtowan and Wadebridge to Owen-nap to see for themselves what we had accomplished. They would be our best salesmen.

Food was already on its way. It may have been hubris, but I was so certain of victory that I had a food train formed and set out before the battles occurred. Once there were full bellies, people would be prone to listen.

Then our head medical person Agnes would arrive with her contingent of nurses. They would start educating the local midwives. They would be our staunchest supporters once they saw how infant death rates could be reduced.

As these events transpired, I thought about how all this started. I was born over a thousand years in the future as James Fletcher. I lived a good life.

Most of it was spent in the military, where I fought in World War II, Korea, and Viet Nam. I was a combat engineer who forgot to duck occasionally and made things happen under fire.

These actions lead to awards and promotions. In between these wars, I continued the engineering studies I had started at West Point. With an eidetic memory, able to retain huge amounts of information. I retired as a Lieutenant General in command of the US Army Corp of Engineers.

During this time, I met, and married the love of my life Dory. She was my helpmate, lover, and confidant for many years. After retiring, I became a professional student. Taking every engineering degree possible. Dory said it kept me off the streets.

I died after living for more than ninety years. That should have been the end. However, as I was fading out, my last thought was, "What a waste of such wonderful knowledge."

Someone must have been listening because I woke up in the body of a young Baron named Owen-nap. The year was the eighth century, and from what I could tell not the same continuum that I came from.

Many things were the same and many different. Why I was here, I had no idea, but I promptly put my engineering knowledge to work to improve the lives of my people.

I had just realized that I needed more people to make progress. Not total body count, but specific trades.

I would need to go to London sometime in the future to recruit them. Number one on my list was an alchemist. They wouldn't know chemistry, but I could remedy that. Their understanding that chemical reactions could change things was a plus.

A master glassmaker was an absolute must. Most important was someone who could lead the effort to measure to the nearest one-thousandth of an inch.

Those were the hard sciences. I also needed someone who knew the geographical world as it exists here. I had seen enough to know that the textbooks I had memorized didn't completely match up with this world.

Then there was a person who knew the nations and politics of this new world, at least new to me.

I also needed a master trader to handle foreign ventures. They would need military support. My list kept growing.

A monk broke me out of my reverie, asking if they could use the Keep as a census headquarters. There was no reason not to, so I gave my permission.

But it raised the question of who I would leave in charge of Pirthtowan and Wadebridge. I was running short of experienced people. I decided to put off that worry until tomorrow. Lady Eleanor would be joining me, and she might have some insight.

At least I wouldn't have to change the title of the Barony again. The Barony of the Middle Counties still worked. Of course, the flag would have to be redesigned.

Then there was the new, to me, surrounding Baronies. Adjacent to Pirthtowan were Lewanniet and Bolventor. Next to Wadebridge were Gaberton and Pensilva.

All these were on the maps I remembered from the future, but none were in the same place. Adding to the evidence that I was in a different timeline or universe.

These differences weren't of much import now but would become critical when I sent out expeditions to bring back raw materials and riches.

In the meantime, I would expand our spy network into these counties. I still hadn't filled the position of spymaster to run a network. It was imperative that this was done soon.

The management team I was building was doing well, but they couldn't do it all. Several were good in their current positions, but the expanded Barony might be beyond them.

I would discuss each person with Eleanor and get her opinion.

My Lady arrived midmorning the next day. She looked exhausted but was almost manic in her excitement. She had never been involved in a war before. War was a strong word for this small-scale battle, but it had changed my Barony and the surrounding countryside.

If war was diplomacy by other means, we had a war.

The Baroness's own accompanied her. I had given up thinking they worked for me. My messenger girl, Linda, came with her. That would be handy. Since it was new territory and we didn't know the inhabitants, I asked Eleanor if one of her guards could accompany her on her missions.

With Thad at my side to take notes and prepare messages and Linda to deliver them, I was all set to go. The question was where to go. Acting too fast would create more problems than solutions. After stabilizing the food and health situation, I should have a complete survey of the area completed before any major changes.

Even hyper Eleanor agreed this was the best course of action. John Steward suggested we assign five guards under a Sergeant to maintain peace in each Barony while we sorted things out. I told him to take care of it.

Rather than dragging Eleanor back on the road, we spent the day in the Wadebridge Keep interviewing the staff. It didn't take long to figure out the Keep's Steward was hated by all. He abused his position. He had disappeared in the fighting and was probably still running for his life. The young serving girls wanted him hunted down.

We didn't waste time on him other than issuing a death warrant if captured. Two girls were seen with knives from the kitchen, checking out hiding spots in the village.

A search of his rooms turned up over three hundred silver coins. I directed ten silver each be distributed to the nine servants. The rest was to go to our treasury.

So far, we have had enough silvers to fund all the ongoing projects, but this state of affairs won't last. A trip to Saltash to speak to John Chandler about establishing more trade with London was in order.

Eleanor and I, with our entourage, returned to Owen-nap. We arrived in the afternoon and received updates on how our orders were being implemented. The next morning, our group headed to Wendon.

Neither Eleanor nor I had been to Wendon since the deaths of the Dowager Baroness and her son. Sergeant Smith was still in charge. He and the Dowager had seemed to be getting very close, so I was concerned about how he was handling things.

'The changes were very apparent. What had been a forlorn-looking village was now a vibrant operation. Healthy-looking people were going about their daily business. Cheers went up as Eleanor and I were spotted.

We waved as we passed by them but didn't stop. Several Monks and a scout peeled off from our group to talk to those present. They would find out the true mood of the people and any concerns they might have.

It may be cynical, but what I hear in public may not be said privately.

Sergeant Smith and the Keep's Steward welcomed us as we arrived at the Keep.
The Sergeant looked like he hadn't been sleeping well.

When Eleanor and I were in a private room with him, I asked how he was bearing up.

"It has been hard, My Lord. I didn't realize how much I cared for her and her son. I have lost many close friends in battle, so I know time will heal."

"It's never easy. Do you want to remain in charge here or go elsewhere?"

"I would like to remain here. Lydia, young William, and I spent many an hour talking about how using your methods could improve Wendon. I would like to continue those efforts in their memory."

"So be it. You will remain in command here. With no heirs, I will incorporate Wendon into the Barony of the Middle Counties."

"I thought as much. You have no choice now."

"Eleanor was talking on the trip over about the command structure here. Leaving a mere Sergeant in charge won't do. I'm Knighting you."

At that, I reached over and lightly tapped his shoulder.

"Now isn't the time to have a big ceremony. We will make it more formal later, Sir Smith."

It was the first time I had seen the former Sergeant taken aback.

A dazed-looking Sir Smith said, "Thank you, My Lord and Lady, I never thought this day would arrive."

"I'm sorry it had to come like this," I replied. "This promotion will also go to Sergeant Waters at Bodmin and those successful in the former Baronies of Pirthtowan and Wadebridge."

Eleanor added, "it is early in your grief, but please look out for those who will trip you and land under you."

"I will be careful of those women."

"Who said it was only women?" Eleanor smirked.

The old Knight blushed.

"Aye, you have the right of it, My Lady."

We spent several hours discussing the specific current needs of the Barony. They were fewer than I thought. Sir Smith and the Dowager had been busy and taken to heart all the new improvements.

I told him of my concerns about the Barons surrounding Pirthtowan and Wadebridge. He had spent time with them and gave some insight into their conditions. It wasn't encouraging.

I could see more warfare in our future. The question now was, should I wait for others to start it or be proactive?

Chapter 2

War was in the future. My immediate concern was to integrate the Middle Counties.

I called what was beginning to be my brain trust together. The people that I had come to lean on and, more importantly, trust.

This group comprised Eleanor, John Steward, Tom Smith, John Chandler, Abbott Luke, and Father Timothy.

Thad was taking notes with Linda Runner stationed outside the door to run errands if needed. The door was guarded by Sara Farmer, head of the Baroness's Own, responsible for the Keep's security.

James Stone was a recent addition to the group for at least this meeting. He was the senior supervisor of the Owen-nap Road building crews.

Eleanor and I had decided the first step in unifying the new larger Barony was to create a road network. I remembered back home that one could tell one had crossed a political boundary because of the changes in the road surface. All the roads in one county would be made to the same specification, but others would be different.

You could tell well-to-do counties by their road types and conditions. I explained this to the gathered group. Not about my previous timeframe, but the common roads identified a community.

After many hours of discussion and several breaks, we concluded there would be three common levels of roads put into place.

The first level would be the major roads connecting the Keep of each of the former Baronies. These would be four lanes wide, two in each direction, with a median between them, much like the interstate highways from my time.

There would be turnout areas for camping and, ultimately, wayside inns.

These would be all-weather roads with good drainage so commerce could continue year-round. We took lessons from the Romans; the roads would have a deep foundation, but we would pour concrete as the top surface.

There would be bridges over any stream, sturdy, with stone piers supporting the ends and each span. There would be no fording at any point.

Drainage would be achieved by ditches with culverts collecting the water and dumping it into retention ponds.

All trees and brush along the road would be trimmed back so that ambushes would be difficult.

This plan was ambitious. The surveying of the routes would take several months. The road building itself would require at least two years.

That was with road crews working from Owen-nap, Saltash, Bodmin, Wendon, Pirthtowan, and Wadebridge.

New mines, crushers, and kilns would have to be opened to provide the needed limestone. And the kilns would need local coal.

The introduction of horse-drawn road scrapers with iron-faced blades by James Stone would help immensely. They were similar to the Fresno Road Scrapers from my time. This invention was why James was now the Superintendent of Roads of the Middle Counties.

James would have a staff of inspectors to track each crew's work. No standing around on this project. He would be headquartered in Owen-nap, which was becoming the area's capital.

Eleanor and I had also debated using Saltash as the Capitol. Owen-nap won out over the larger Saltash because of its central location.

The secondary roads would be similar to the first level roads, but they would only have one lane with frequent turnouts. Like the first level, they would have a concrete surface and all-weather drainage.

They would go from Keep to each village or major work area. Mines and mills would rate the secondary roads.

As things progressed, traffic would dictate which roads would be upgraded to two lanes.

The third-level roads would go from village to individual holdings. These roads would be scraped earth, covered in gravel. As time, traffic, and money permitted, they would be upgraded to secondary roads.

Not wanting to get too bogged down in details, I set up a subcommittee comprised of James Stone, Tom Smith, Father Timothy, and Eleanor to develop the support needed to build the roads.

We needed an estimate of the manpower required and the tools, such as picks and shovels. Then there were heavier machines like scrapers and rollers to compact the earth and gravel and a myriad of wagons.

Oxen or horses would be needed to pull the wagons along with drivers. And they would need food and water. Fortunately, we wouldn't have to haul water to many locations as streams were abundant.

People needed to be fed, so chuck wagons had to be provided. They were used to either bringing their food or working hungry, but I calculated they would work more efficiently if I ensured they had adequate nutrition.

The routes need to be surveyed, so our surveying crews would be busy.

And this would all require money. While the treasury was in good shape, it wasn't unlimited.

Eleanor gave me a nasty look but didn't say anything. I suspect we will have a conversation in our room tonight. She feels the same way about committees as I do. They are tools of the devil.

Several days later and many mea culpas, I was at the Monastery to see how they were coming on the book projects, particularly those I had been dictating.

Walking through the main copying area, I heard a young Monk chastised because his lines weren't level. They were straight but at an angle.

I stopped out of curiosity and found the problem as described. The lines were straight because the young man used a straight edge but hadn't kept it parallel with the preceding lines.

The copyist was working at a small desk with no angle to it. I couldn't help but make a suggestion or two.

"There would be fewer errors if he had a T-square available."

"What's a T-square, My Lord?"

It was simple to explain how one worked.

"We should make the working surface larger and adjustable to different angles while at it. May I borrow this young man for a while? I want to take him to the cabinetmaker and arrange for one to be built?"

"You may have this young lout forever, as far as I'm concerned."

Forgetting my original mission, the young man and I proceeded to the cabinetmaker's shop. On the way, I quizzed him about his time as a junior Monk. Without directly saying it, I could tell he hated it.

William Farmer was a bright and personable young man, and I saw a lot of promise in him. Monastic life was a waste of his talents.

Mark Woodson came to my side as soon as we entered his shop. Strange how they always had time for me when I needed it.

Several sketches later, the drafting board was born a thousand years early. The T-square, a right triangle, and a thirty-degree triangle accompanied it.

It was a shame that we didn't have clear plastic, but thin wood would do the trick.

Woodson even figured out a way to adjust the drafting table without using any of the metal we needed for so many other projects, using a ratcheted wooden support over a dowel to shift the table's angle about 7 degrees at a time.

A drawer would hold the drafting tools.

From there, we segued into a drawing cabinet. I told William that he was to work with Master Woodson to find the best table height. It would even need a special stool.

"I see these as possible items to be manufactured and sold in London. Pay attention, and we may get you out of the Monastery and into sales or production."

He brightened up at these prospects and made arrangements with Mark to be available every step of the way.

I wrote a note to his supervising monk saying the young lout was now mine forever. If this project didn't pan out, I had many other uses for him.

The hardest part of the drafting table project was the wingnut on the adjustment slide. The thread count was critical to how easy it would be to adjust the table angle.

No one would want to spend too much time getting the angle just right.

It was a slow process, but we could meet our anticipated needs. How many drafting boards could be needed in London?

Another business venture was starting up. I financed Paul Stableman, who was in charge of the Keep's stables, in starting a haulage company between the former Baronies, now known as Districts.

It was our version of UPS. The only difference was that the wagons would take animals in crates from one District to another, plus the normal packages and correspondence.

Paul took service to a new level when he allowed drunks to mail themselves home. This was not to be confused with a taxi service. The drunks were treated as a package, tossed into the back of the wagon, and delivered by the same method.

No one mailed themselves twice. Paul also had a transportation wagon with multiple seats. It even had a roof to keep the rain off. I wondered what good that was on the open-sided wagon.

But it did move people from one District to another with relative ease. Before, they would have had to walk. Few chose to do that, as bandits had been a problem.

There were no bandits to speak of these days. My armsmen patrolled the roads. Besides, we had full employment, which helped more than the patrols.

I had considered setting up a system of semaphore towers between the districts.

Unfortunately, we don't have usable telescopes yet. Working out the cost of towers and crews without the advantage of telescopes made them too expensive.

And while we had copper, it seemed too soon for our technical base to set up a telegraph system. That was probably several years away.

I did have a Pony Express system set up for carrying urgent news. This system was for emergencies only, like being invaded. Runs were made once a month to keep the system as a viable option. It was like testing the emergency broadcast system.

Our mounted troops made the runs, which were a new addition to our forces. It didn't take long for the rides to become a contest. Once riders were competing against each other, gambling followed.

Crude clocks were sealed in a pouch so they couldn't be tampered with. A few bets between riders were okay. But when the general public became involved, corruption worked its way in.

I had the people involved in the first fixing of the races hanged. Then, I forbade the carrying of clocks.

The newspaper made a big deal out of covering the story. There was an official editorial supporting my actions. An op-ed also stated I was taking the fun out of life.

My first reaction was to hang the op-eds author, but I loved Eleanor too much for that. It did open up a conversation about allowing some Barony-wide events and even officially sanctioned gambling.

I returned to the Monastery a week later to see the new drafting table. They called it the drawing table, but a rose is a rose by any other name. Right?

The woodworking part of it was magnificent. This was made like a piece of furniture to be handed down for generations.

The ones from my first life were nice but had a commercial, made-in-a-factory look. This table looked crude only when you looked underneath to see the tilting mechanism.

It was functional but didn't have the smooth look of machine-cast parts. More like a piece hammered out by a blacksmith. Surprise.

William Farmer proudly showed me how the T-square and triangles worked together. The lip on the T-square to prevent ink from flowing underneath was like an eighth wonder of the world to him.

His supervisor wanted to know how soon I could replace their work desks with these wonderful devices. I told him the Abbott had to order and negotiate the prices with Mark Woodson.

This one was a gift. The Monastery had to buy others.

Chapter 3

The road network would have mile markers, which would be the basis for surveying property boundaries. The stone zero-mile maker was at the well in Owen-nap. It was the tallest at ten feet. All the others were six feet tall.

Unfortunately, the tall zero marker became known as the Baron's Prick. I hated it, but Eleanor would giggle every time she saw it.

I'm glad I didn't make it shorter than the others.

The mile markers and the attendant surveys would take several years. As each section of the Barony was surveyed, a map would be updated. The written record would prevent the tragedy of enclosure at a later date.

The maps created were listed as a state secret, and few were allowed access.

That meant the first person to request access was the new Advocate. His client was in a boundary feud. When the request came to me for approval, I sent a new set of surveyors out to reconfirm the boundaries.

The farmer trying to claim his neighbor's land was charged for the survey. That was the last time anyone tried to steal land through the use of a lawyer. Did I mention I disliked lawyers, even while recognizing their need in certain cases?

While all this was going on, there was a full-blown census being carried out in the Baronies that had just been added.

This census not only did a headcount but listed all major farm animals and known raw material deposits on the land.

One of my trips took me back to the leather works. Things still weren't moving fast enough for me. The bellows for the blast furnace were still a month or more away.

For some reason, my funny memory brought up a book that I had read many years ago. Why I thought of it, I don't know, but I did.

My mind was like a library. I had to think of a specific book to open it. In this case, I had almost forgotten the book existed.

When I 'opened' the book, it had descriptions of two very useful technologies, I brought them up in our brain trust meetings.

The first was a method of compressing air without electricity.

This method depended on water falling far enough into sealed chambers. The rapidly falling water compresses the air in the chambers. The air can then be piped away to provide compressed air for various uses.

With two or more such chambers, you can have a fairly steady flow of compressed air, and unlike most air compression mechanisms, this does not heat the air as it is compressed. It absorbs and carries away the heat. This procedure was used in drilling one of the early Alpine tunnels.

The second device was a Ram pump to lift water. Known as trompes, they are very simple devices. They consist of four main parts: a water supply pipe or shaft with an air inlet inside it, a water outflow pipe, a separation chamber, and a takeoff air pipe.

The vertical pipe or shaft goes down from a higher point to a separation chamber. A pipe typically narrower than the previous one, coming away from that chamber, allows the water to exit at a lower level, and another pipe (air pipe) coming from the chamber allows the compressed air to exit as needed.

Water rushing down the vertical pipe falls through a constriction. The constriction produces a lower pressure, the venturi effect, and an external port allows air to be sucked in, thus creating a constant air supply.

The air forms bubbles in the pipe. As the bubbles go down the pipe, they are pressurized proportionally to the hydraulic head, which is the height of the column of water in the pipe. The compressed air rises to the top of the separation chamber (wind box). The separation chamber has a compressed air takeoff pipe, and the compressed air can be used as a power source.

We could raise a water column about seventy percent of the height of the device. We could use this in combination with the air compressor in our blast furnace to replace the bellows, and fill water towers for each Keep, village, and even individual farms if they had streams nearby.

I rounded up my brain trust as I thought of them. After explaining the devices, the questions came.

Eleanor started. "James, what is this venturi effect you talk of?"

"Are you aware that liquid water can't be compressed?"

"Do you take me for an idiot, dear husband?"

The dangerous ground here!

"No, dear, I just want to be certain we all have the same understanding of the nature of water."

"Okay, continue."

"Think of the stream where the battle of Bodmin occurred. Near the battle site, the water flow is slow and peaceful. Further downstream, it narrows and flows faster. As you know, these are rapids. There water moves faster since the water can't be compressed when the banks narrow.

"When the banks widen, the water flows slower. This change in speed of flow by constricting the width of the stream gives the venturi effect. Now imagine if we used a pipe with a wide opening and then narrowed it down. The water pressure would be greater because the same amount of water is pushing against a smaller area."

I had come prepared for this with twelve tubes. Half of them had a much larger diameter than the other. I had them take a mouthful of water and blow it through the tubes. The larger tube spilled into their laps. The smaller shot across the room.

While they got the point, my humor wasn't appreciated. Abbott Luke mumbled about respecting one's elders. Eleanor called me a brat.

I didn't go into the air pressure differential as they didn't need to know, and I was uncertain how to demonstrate it.

"Next, I would like to demonstrate that, unlike water, air can be compressed."

For this demonstration, I had a crude hypodermic syringe made. There was no needle, just a small plugged hole at the end. When the injector was pressed down, it compressed the air.

The airflow out of the hole could be seen on a feather I held in front of it.

Father Timothy stated, "This is the venturi effect once more."

I plugged the hole back up and recharged the syringe. After letting it sit for a minute, I unplugged the hole, and all could see the air rushing out as the feather moved.

I then refilled the syringe with water and performed the same action. When pressed, the water flowed out in a stream.

"This is water being pushed through a constriction. Now watch. I'll push the injector as far as I can. Since water can't be compressed, it will stop. The water will stream out when I pull the plug at the bottom."

Performing that action, it streamed as predicted.

"Now, let's put the plug back in and press the injector. Instead of pulling the plug immediately, we will let it sit. Since there will be no pressure pushing on the water, it will not flow faster."

When I pulled the plug, the water came out slowly.

"Compressed air stays at the same pressure as long as it is contained. We will have the water raised to fall and compress the air using the ram pump. The falling water will compress the air. Two of them will provide more air than the bellows, and as Tom knows, the higher pressure will make the flame burn hotter.

"Why is that?" asked John Steward.

Tom answered, "The fire needs air. The more you give it, the hotter it burns. To stop a fire, we cut off the air supply with a heavy blanket."

Father Timothy said, "So, when did you learn these 'natural laws,' as you call them?"

"I don't know. I was at the tanner's, and suddenly, the thoughts were in my mind."

"I don't see how this could be the devil's work. Yet I have never heard of God working in this manner."

I replied, "but doesn't the good book say God moves in mysterious ways?"

"Not directly, but you have a point."

Fortunately, the conversation moved on to building a practical device. Tom would assign two apprentices that were better trained to build it under his supervision. It would be their journeyman project.

Abbott Luke, of course, wanted to print a book. We convinced him to wait until we had a finished device so illustrations could be made.

I wasn't sure if we wanted to share this knowledge now. It had both tactical and strategic benefits. We estimated it would take two months if all went well. It hadn't yet. There was always something, but one could hope.

Thad brought up an interesting point.

"Could the glass blowers use this compressed air? I notice the men have to take many breaks, as they only have so much breath."

I almost jumped for joy. "Thad, you are a genius. Of course, they can blow glass with compressed air."

Our glass house had three furnaces. The first, which holds a crucible of molten glass, is simply referred to as "the furnace." The second is called the "glory hole" and is used to reheat a piece in between steps of working with it. The final furnace is called the "lehr" or "annealer" and is used to slowly cool the glass over a period of a few hours to a few days, depending on the size of the pieces. This keeps the glass from cracking or shattering due to thermal stress.

We had the major tools used by a glassblower. The blowpipe, mandrel, bench, marver, blocks, jacks, paddles, tweezers, pads, and various shears.

The tip of the blowpipe is first preheated; then dipped in the molten glass in the furnace. The molten glass is "gathered" onto the end of the blowpipe in much the same way that viscous honey is picked up on a honey dipper. This glass is then rolled on the marver, a flat slab of marble.

This process, called "marvering," forms a cool skin on the exterior of the molten glass blob and shapes it. Then the air is blown into the pipe, creating a bubble. Next, the glassworker can gather more glass over that bubble to create a larger piece.

The bottom is finalized once a piece has been blown to its approximate final size. Then, the molten glass is attached to a stainless steel or iron rod called a mandrel for shaping and transferring the hollow piece from the blowpipe to provide an opening and finalize the top.

There are many ways to apply patterns and color to blown glass, including rolling molten glass in powdered color or larger pieces of colored glass called "frit." Complex patterns with great detail can be created through the use of cane (rods of colored glass) and murrine (rods cut in cross-sections to reveal patterns).

These pieces of color can be arranged in a pattern on a flat surface and then "picked up" by rolling a bubble of molten glass over them. One of the most exacting and complicated caneworking techniques is "reticello," which involves creating two bubbles from a cane, each twisted in a different direction, then combining them and blowing out the final form.

The people in the glasshouse knew about the techniques. I gave them the names from a book on glassmaking I had memorized. I was surprised to learn these techniques had been known for hundreds of years, just not in our backwater.

Having compressed air would enable us to increase the production of molded pieces dramatically. No more extended breaks for our glassblowers. Since I owned the glasshouse, my profits would go up. I had to remember to share these with the workers.

We could increase the production of plates, saucers, and goblets immediately. More molds would be needed, but they were the least of my worries.

I got so lost in thought that my brain trust left me sitting at the table.

Chapter 4

I could kick myself. I had forgotten a book that gave us compressed air for our blast furnaces, glassmaking, and other uses. Yet there was an easy way to find out what books I had read that might be useful.

As a special student of many years at MIT, I was given some unusual freedoms. One of those was permission to the Hayden library stacks. Of course, I hadn't read all the books, but when I pictured the shelves in my mind, I would try to open a book.

I browsed my mental remembrance of the areas which touched on historical engineering. Over the course of my almost forty years at MIT, I have written many papers and used a great number of books.

Like most people, I first checked the index for the subjects I was interested in and specifically looked at those pages. That meant that while I had many of those books in hand, or in mind, in this case, I hadn't read them, so I couldn't bring them up.

Even so, I found many useful books.

One had a history of developing the first measuring instruments. I was interested in how to measure to the nearest thousandths of an inch. Fortunately, it had been a reference in one of my many papers.

We had to make gauge blocks or, as some called them, jo blocks. I wouldn't introduce that term. I talked to Tom and his apprentice, explaining that I had remembered a different approach.

Making sets of gauge blocks that could be used for precision measurements in all the shops was a necessary first step in cutting or machining accurately in wood or metal, but we really needed adjustable fine measuring tools, like micrometers, or as close as we could get.

For some reason, the design and building of such devices had never been part of my extensive engineering and science education. They were always just assumed, like axioms in plane geometry.

I had to reason from first principles instead. I knew that with the gauge blocks and existing tooling, I could make a consistently reproducible large measurement of about a quarter inch. I never could sell the metric system and had given up.

To make reproducible adjustable measurements, I was going to need screw threads. They would have to be cut accurately in metal. The key was to make up a bunch of cutting heads of the hardest steel I could forge and spend time getting those as nearly identical as I could manage.

Then, working from one gauge block for consistency and using simple geometry, I'd cut a set of gears with ten teeth each, and use those to advance at a steady rate a cutting head to cut a large thread around a one-inch diameter brass rod.

Once I had a brass rod a couple of feet long with ten threads to the inch, I could use that and the gears to advance a cutting head around another brass rod at 100 threads to the inch. The rods had to be brass at this stage so that my steel tools could cut them, though even brass required frequent replacement of cutting heads.

Once I had the gears and the threaded rods, I could use them to make more threaded rods, but the first set would be the standard. As soon as I could, I would make up a set of rods and gears in steel for permanence, and they'd be the new standard.

Using our new magnifying lenses, the accuracy and consistency of the thread count with either metal were checked with the smallest gauge blocks we had.

With accurately threaded rods and gears, it would be simple to adjust a cutting head on a lathe to a tolerance of a thousandth of an inch and even move the tool along the object being turned by similar tolerances.

We could start producing drill presses and other accurate machine tools, but they would all need threaded rods and accurately cut gears, so producing the tooling to make the rods and gears consistently and the "tools to make the tools" was the key.

Then take the tooling part to an inch block and measure the part to be cut. Take a 1/8 or 1/10 block to measure threads randomly. Set up the cutting machine with gears that turn the rod 100 times for each inch it advances. You may have to run the rod through the cutter multiple times to cut the grooves deep enough.

To complete the micrometer you build from this, you need a mating hollow cylinder grooved on the inside with cut grooves corresponding to the ones on the rod. Advancing the rod 1 inch per hundred turns is the easy part.

Holding the cutting head in the right position, and keeping it the right size, shape, and hardness throughout the cutting process, is the hard part.

To minimize drag and heat buildup, you're going to do most of the cutting in a flax oil bath, which will do a lot to extend the life of our cutting heads. The first time we cut will primarily be to establish a wear rate on our cutting heads, so we know how often to change them.

It's a shame olive oil isn't being imported from Rome anymore. It was a better lubricant than flax oil, but we had to work with what we had. To my knowledge, we didn't have any open oil seeps, and the chemistry to get oil out of coal tars was far beyond us.

Now that I had this wonderful mental breakthrough, the gauge blocks and screw rods had to be made. That would probably take the better part of this year.

Then there was manufacturing enough tools to be useful, and training a workforce in their use.

Aside from my work with the Smiths, I had many other irons in the fire. One of my plans was to have an icehouse in each District. I was trying not to think of them as Baronies anymore but as subsets of my Barony of the Middle Counties.

I ignored the fact that calling it the Middle Counties suggested I might be a Count. I wasn't ready to put that big of a target on my back.

The problem with an icehouse in every District was the need for a place to store the ice. In Owen-nap, I was able to take advantage of a cavern in a convenient location.

All the others had caverns of various sizes, but all were in the wrong place. Ice houses must be built in each District with poured concrete walls. These would be double walls with air space to act as insulation.

To enter would require passing through a triple-doored hallway large enough for wagons, with only one door open at a time.

The one in Saltash would be enormous as the town was more than twice the size of all the others.

We had to erect longhouses in each District to house students and schoolrooms. Boys and girls would be in separate buildings. We had learned that lesson.

Then there was ensuring that there was safe drinking water. This included wells or aqueducts and sewage systems. Plans were drawn up for a real sewage system instead of nightsoil collection. Owen-nap, as the most advanced, would receive the first system. Saltash, as the largest with the most housing and poorly laid roads, would be the last.

I authorized the building of Inns or Taverns by private enterprise. Our workforce was only so large. Let private enterprises pick up the slack.

Not to give the impression that it was all work and no play, Eleanor and I spent some nice evenings together. Besides the expected, I read to her. The libraries I browsed had fiction sections, and I brought some books home.

I read several different novels to her that I remembered word for word. I found that she had a taste for steamy romances. My late wife Dory also had that taste, which is why I read them. Sure.

What I didn't know was that we had eavesdroppers. In their roles as maids Marion and Anne had to be close by to attend to Eleanor's needs. That was their story, and they were sticking to it. We wouldn't have known they were listening in if Anne hadn't sneezed.

After that, they joined the readings openly. The three ladies enjoyed discussing each character and how they acted. To make the story understandable, I changed cars to carriages and TVs to fireplaces, among other things.

Even so, there were several awkward discussions. I had to explain what a baby bottle was. Once they understood, there was an immediate demand for me to introduce them locally. It meant that the men could feed the child during the night!

I might end up getting stoned to death by all the husbands.

Things grew from there. The maids started sharing the stories with their friends. Before you knew it, both maids were taking notes as I read. I wasn't surprised when stories started showing up in our newspaper.

When that first appeared, I realized I needed less steam and more romance. I tried that for a while until Father Timothy asked me why the stories were becoming boring. I had forgotten how bawdy this age was.

Abbott Luke got into the act. He asked permission to print books with the stories. I said yes, but realized they would need some careful editing. No flying machines or light bulbs. Dishwashers would be scullery maids.

I dedicated half an hour daily to reading a new chapter with scribes capturing it all. It hadn't occurred to me to do that with the technical manuals and textbooks I was transcribing, so there was a benefit from all this.

I even thought about introducing the rotary press but realized that it was beyond our technical capabilities at this time.

Abbott Luke solved the problem by commissioning three new presses to be built and a new building to house the printing operations.

The most popular story I read to the ladies was Sir Henry Fielding's 'Tom Jones.' It was bawdy, but not as raw as some books I had read. Those books wouldn't have bothered my audience, but they left me blushing.

At the rate we were going, we would need to build a paper mill. The local hand operations had a hard time keeping up. When we started shipping books to London, we would need a lot of paper and ink.

Not an immediate problem, but a growing concern. I had spent a lot of silver, and if things didn't change by the middle of next year, I would have to cut back.

Cutting back meant putting school and road projects on hold. They didn't produce income in the short term, but long-term growth would be endangered without them.

I would have to make a trip to London later this year or early next to see what new trade deals might be set up. A trip to London brought about a new set of concerns. Here I was, a big deal. There I was nothing. I could be made to disappear, and no one there would worry.

Why anyone would do this, I don't know, but it was something to think about. I had to figure- out how to accomplish the trip without making waves.

Word had come back through John Chandlers, people who went back and forth to London, that Saltash was being watched carefully as new inventions emanated from there.

I hadn't been identified as the source, but it wouldn't be long before word would trickle out. If nothing else, a copy of our newspaper making its way to London would let the cat out of the bag. Worse yet, it put a big target on my back.

Some would want to conquer me, others kill me, and all would be jealous of what was being built here.

Chapter 5

Speaking of those who might attack. I had to become more familiar with the surrounding Baronies. There were more Baronies of concern other than the ones adjacent to Pirthtowan and Wadebridge. However, those were the most critical at this time.

There was a need for a file on each of them. Including the number of troops maintained, their weapons, training levels, trained reserves, if any, etc.

Layouts of each Keep, road system, and the state of food supplies would be needed. Then a profile of each Baron and their family. Also, any alliances they have or important connections with the powers in London.

I set this in motion for Polventor, Lewanniet, Pensilva, and Gaberton. Interestingly, I had seen books with maps of modern and ancient Cornwall.

There was a long list of contingent Baronies now. There would be more as we expanded. I realized that the stronger my possessions became, the more tempting a target they were. This seemed to set up an almost endless cycle. Would I have to conquer the world to have peace?

Not on my to-do list, which was for sure.

The next most critical Barony to pay attention to was Looe. It was located between Pirthtowan and Bodmin to their north. It could attack either one.

Looe was on my list of Unknowns. They might be the most peaceful people around, but I needed a first read on them and dispatched scouts to perform a surface investigation.

Further north of Bodmin was Padstow. It was not as much of a concern as the Brunwenely Hills were between them and Bodmin. It would take invaders several days to circle around. Even so, a file was started on them.

Bude and Caustock were west and southwest of Wendon. They had made no moves against Wendon, but again, I needed to know their situation.

East and west of Saltash were Redruth and Fowey. They had been trading peacefully through Saltash long before I came on the scene, and I didn't think they would be a problem. Still, they were on my list to investigate.

Then there were Hilston and Liskeard. Both were northwest of Wendon. The Brunwenely Hills were between Wendon and them. Still, I needed to know. They would be the last on my list to investigate.

I hoped to have a first look at them by the end of summer. After the harvests were in would be the danger time.

Then there were the Brunwenely Hills themselves. From what I could gather, they were avoided by most people. There were rumors of strange happenings at the two cairns on top of the Mountain.

I wasn't superstitious and wondered if there were any veins of ore to be found on the hill. To me, it was a high hill, to the locals, a mountain.

A mining crew was dispatched to the hill area with orders to look for possible ores in the southeast quadrant of the area. This would keep them away from the adjacent Baronies.

I didn't want to start anything with them, so I felt it was best to keep our distance.

When the first spy/scouts returned from checking out those next to Pirthtowan and Wadebridge, they had an answer to my question.

"Were they planning on invading us."

The answer was a resounding, "No. Maybe. We don't know."

There were no overt signs of preparing for war. But at this time of year, there wouldn't be. The troops would be assembled in the fall.

They observed messengers shuttling back and forth between the four Baronies. More than one would expect.

They could be in the planning stages for war or a huge harvest festival. We would have to embed people with them to get a better idea.

My people were getting better at this spy business. It only took several weeks to have people wander into the larger villages and take up work in public places like Inns and Taverns. It would be slow going, but they would find out what the planning was all about.

In the meantime, I detailed the scouts to find areas along the trail to each of the four Baronies that would be good battle spaces. For us, that is.

They identified spots for Pensilva and Bolventor that were perfect. There was no need for any battlefield preparation. Hand-drawn maps of the area made it easy for us to make our battle plan.

Areas for troops were designated. The actual battlefield would be staked out to show each unit where they would be placed. This would occur just before the battle, so no one would accidentally stumble across them.

Lewanniet and Gaberton had several possible sites, but they would need some improvements, such as a small bridge at one stream and a staircase up a steep hill in the other.

With my combat engineering experience, designing a portable bridge for the stream was easy. The staircase parts would be brought in as a kit. Troops could dig out the flats for the staircase boards and install handrails in no time.

I had learned the hard way to have handrails on both sides to accommodate right and left-handed people.

Being late spring, with planting just finishing, it was a good time to take inventory of our forces.

At this time, I had thirty crossbowmen and twenty men at arms. When I had gone against Wadebridge, it was with thirty-five men. After taking Wade and Pirth, as the troops called them, we recruited from their villages.

From what information we could gather, the new four, as my brain trust called them, had seventy-five men at arms and twenty bowmen.

It was easy to train a crossbowman, but almost a lifetime for an archer.

We needed more soldiers but had seemly tapped out the available manpower. That is until my good wife reminded me that we hadn't touched our woman power.

Though the US Army hadn't allowed women onto the battlefield, at least in my day. I had seen what women could do. From French partisans to Viet Cong fighters, they got the job done. I would stack the Israeli women against any army in the world.

Our first recruiting call netted us over one hundred women. Of those, eighty made it through our basic training.

So now we had a potential army of one hundred and seventy-five soldiers. Not warriors, but still soldiers.

I still fretted about what the four Baronies' intentions were. Eleanor got tired of me questioning things.

She finally said, "Why don't you ask them."

I was flummoxed. It was so obvious! After stuttering around a bit, I admitted that it had never occurred to me.

My recent experiences with the different Baronies had been bad, so I assumed they would all go that way.

I sent an envoy to each of them, inviting a delegation to come to Owen-nap and see what we were doing.

All four of them accepted my offer. None of the Barons came themselves, but I hadn't expected them to. Hostage-taking is an honored tradition in this day and age.

The envoys traveled together. There were two representatives and five men at arms from each Barony. It was an impressive cavalcade that came to Owen-nap.

Since our scouts knew when they left Pensilva, we had a welcoming committee waiting for them.

Somehow a combined regular and reserve forces training day got scheduled at the same time. The soldiers were on a field exercise that happened to be next to the main road from Wade to Owen-nap.

My people accompanying them said nothing, and the envoys pretended not to notice. I bet their escorting soldiers did!

The envoys were richly dressed. Flowing robes over tunic and trousers. The robes were different colors and had an embroidered crest sewn on them. I wasn't familiar with them, assuming they represented each Barony.

The one with a green robe was from Bolventor, Sir Edwin. The red-robed one, Sir Thomas from Lewanniet. The dark blue robe belonged to Sir Lucas from Pensilva. Last was a brown drab-looking robe worn by Sir Stephen of Gaberton.

From the touches of silver in their hair and sun-worn looks, I would guess they were all in their forties. Other than the robes, they were remarkably similar in their looks, medium height, barrel-chested, dark hair, and dark eyes.

As I guessed, they were all advisors to their Barons.

Their guards were well turned out and looked like they knew what they were doing. Each group of five was well aware of its surroundings. I bet they didn't like seeing our field exercises. I think they got the message.

I hope that seeing such power would squash any ideas of invading. Our self-introductions were bland except for Sir Edwin from Bolventor.

He started with, "So you're the Baron who attacked the two lesser Baronies."

"No, I'm the Baron who struck back at an assassination attempt."

"We are to take your word for that?"

"If you please, your opinion doesn't change anything."

"You dare to challenge the mighty Bolventor."

At this point, Sir Stephen of Gaberton broke in.

"I think we are getting off on the wrong foot. Let's start over."

Looking like he had swallowed a lemon, Sir Edwin backed down.

"I apologize if you took what I said amiss."

He wasn't apologizing for his statements. It was my misunderstanding. If it was war, I knew who was going first.

Gaberton. They were the strength of the four.

Publicly I shrugged it off and invited them into my Keep for refreshments. I wanted them to see the surrounding walls and the Keep itself.

The female crossbow women walking the ramparts were also on display. Coincidentally, target practice was going on, and the ladies quickly put bolt after bolt into the center ring.

Yesterday they had a shoot off, and the best was practicing now. Stack the deck? Of course!

After luncheon, I showed the envoys around the village. Sir Thomas commented on how clean it was. I took the opportunity to explain the new sewage system and our water sources. I had to show them both wells within the Keep's walls. I didn't have to, but I wanted to let them know we could withstand a siege.

They voiced appreciation for the grain storage within the walls. I took them to the main storage area for wheat we would be selling this year. They made no comments. I think they were speechless. I informed the Barons that each farm had storage on site to feed them for the year.

The blacksmith shop, tannery, and glass works all had been cleaned up to look their best. The visitors were overwhelmed, so I took them back to our open-air tavern by the main well and bought them a drink.

By design, Abbott Luke dropped by with the latest edition of our newspaper. Sir Thomas wanted to know why we had a newspaper when only a few could read.

Abbott Luke quickly disabused him of this idea because all in the Middle County Baronies were learning to read, write, and do mathematics.

Sir Stephen picked up on the Middle County Baronies.

"I thought this was Owen-nap?"

"It is, but now it is only one District in our Barony."

"What are the others?"

"Wendon, Bodmin, Saltash, and of course, you know of Pirthtowan, and Wadebridge."

Now it was Sir Stephen who looked like he had swallowed a lemon.

After dinner, they were shown to their rooms in the Keep. They were even allowed to have two of their guards at their door. The others were given bunks in the barracks.

I was looking forward to tomorrow. The Knights still had to be shown the mining operations and sit through a presentation by Agnes on health care and mortality rates. Then there was the road system.

When we were done, they would want what we had, but would know they couldn't take it.

Chapter 6

I headed to the blacksmith shop several days later at a brisk walk. Tom Smith sent me a message asking for a meeting at his shop.

I was the one that called meetings and summoned people. Being summoned had never happened before, so I was very curious.

When I entered the room, Tom Smith, Simon Mason, and Philip Miner were waiting for me. On a slab table in front of me were samples of the iron and lime we were turning out.

"Look at this shite! My Lord!" said Smith. "We're getting plenty of iron now from the smelters you've set up, but the iron is of poor quality, spongy, and full of impurities. Which require a great deal of time and effort in the forge to clean up."

He continued, "With all your new projects, we need a better grade of iron to meet our needs."

I've heard similar stories from Philip here about the lime we are turning out and Mason, the brickyard operator. We have ample quantity, but the quality leaves much to be desired!"

"What do you suggest we do about it, Smith?" I asked, knowing full well the answer. I had been putting this off because of the cost involved. I wasn't made of silver.

"My Lord, I suspect the problem is that none of our furnaces can get hot enough to purify the materials we're refining or bake the bricks hard. The coal we're burning turns to black smoke up the chimneys and rains down all around. I don't think it's burning completely, as what doesn't go up the chimney comes out as lumps in the ashes when we bank the fires."

He was right. It is incomplete combustion. We're wasting fuel and not getting enough heat for what we're burning.

"My Lord, we have to spend some coin to improve the heat we generate if we are going to have the quality we need to make real steel and be cost-effective."

Again, he was correct, and though my pocketbook complained loudly, I knew the investments had to be made. Once more, I was reminded that these people were ignorant in some situations. But they weren't as backward as I sometimes thought and not close to being stupid.

I said, "Simon, come see me. I have some new kinds of bricks that might help."

"How are the new water chambers to compress air for the furnaces working? Are they not making the fires hotter? And with less labor?"

"The quality from those furnaces is better, My Lord, but still not as good as we need."

That tears it, I thought. We would have to rework the furnaces and the air supplies to get hotter temperatures. The blast furnaces may require something else.

Mason inquired. "When, My Lord?"

"Right after this meeting, let's go to your yard. I want you to bake more clay pipes, and on some of them, you need to taper just the ends, the last foot, or so, of the pipes, down to a third of their usual diameter."

"What's this for, if I may ask, My Lord?" he responded.

"We need enough pipes to direct more air, at least one pipe with a tapered end in each square yard of the furnace interiors. We must push more air into the furnaces to make them burn hotter. Tapering the air pipes will speed the air and force it deeper in the kilns and furnaces."

"Very well, My Lord. Shall I prepare the brick linings for more compression tanks, too? And will you divert another stream to supply water to flood the tanks?"

He is a bright fellow.

"Good thinking, Mason. Make it so!"

Turning back to Tom, I continued, "we need to divert some of the lime supply to the blast furnaces to replace the crushed limestone we've been putting in with the iron ore and coal.

"The increased efficiency of the improved lime kilns should prevent a shortfall in lime production, and I think you'll find that by using lime, even bad lime, instead of limestone, and by making the furnaces hotter, we'll get purer iron, purer lime, and harder bricks!"

I could see that my last statements had Philip dancing in place.

"Yes, Philip?"

"My Lord, we won't be able to keep up with the needs for good lime if we do this."

"I know we will need more limestone operations to keep up. Plan a limestone mine and kiln operation in every District in the next six months. That is the only way we can build our highways."

"That will cost a fortune!"

I mentally groaned but didn't show it outwards.

"That is my problem to handle. Yours is to provide the lime."

I had to appear confident to my followers, or they would lose heart. This was the same as leading troops in combat. Raising money was much easier, and no one was shooting at me. At least yet.

Simon, "Let's go over to the brickyard, and I will show you what I want in the pipes."

"Maybe we should go to the new drafting table in the Monastery and make a drawing so production will know what we need. I gather this will use that venturi effect you demonstrated the other day?"

As I said, ignorance is not the same as stupidity.

"Good thinking."

I turned to Tom and Philip, "When Simon has the tubes available, you must build new kilns and furnaces. It will be less costly than reworking the current ones. I am sure that we will have some uses for them."

Tom and Philip looked at each other.

Tom spoke up, "We can get a head start by laying the foundations for the new works. Tearing down the old kilns and furnaces would save time and cost if we used their materials to build the new ones."

He continued, "You realize we will need at least twice the new air compression capacity."

"Yes, start on that now."

My poor treasury would be like Mother Hubbard's cupboard.

These changes would slow production until the furnaces were all reworked, but speed up production overall and, in the long run, with better quality.

That evening, I related all to Eleanor.

She had a grin as she listened.

"What's so funny?"

"They knew the answers before you got there. You have been played, my dear."

After my small flare of anger, I had to laugh a little.

"And well played at that!"

"Of course, this means I will have to go to London sooner than later to find ways to make more silver."

"Oh, a shopping trip, I will love it!"

In my many years of marriage, I had learned when to keep my mouth shut.

One product that I knew would make money for us was optics. First, reading stones, then eyeglasses, and finally, telescopes.

The reading stones were simple concave lenses for short-sightedness or convex for farsightedness.

They would be laid flat on the surface needing magnification, such as a page being written by a Monk.

Most Monks had to stop copying by age forty because their eyes had changed.

We would make blanks and carve or work them to different curvatures. These different curvatures would give a selection of different strengths. Like an eyeglass store, people could try the different strengths to see which worked best for them.

These would be easy to make, well, easy compared to a telescope.

The raw material we would have to use was calcined flint from around the cliffs of Dover. This was the best for optics compared to the soda lime we now had.

John Chandler did me the favor of bringing ten tons of the stuff back from London. He was interested enough to ask what I wanted it for. When I explained it, he wanted the franchise to sell the reading stones.

The initial run of stones would be ten of each of the five powers for nearsightedness and the same for farsightedness.

He would have a salesman take them to the major Monastery in the London area and demonstrate them to the Monks for sale. He would take orders for later delivery if he sold more than these. The initial price would be ten silver per stone.

The Monks themselves couldn't afford them, but the Monastery could. It was going to be interesting to see how that played out.

I had read a book on the curvatures of lenses so we could produce drawings (with the help of William Farmer) of what was needed. Once the lenses were made to specification and polished, we identified people needing various powers. They would be our quality control.

The glassblowers at my direction experimented with adding lead in small quantities to the calcined flint. They then would melt the thoroughly mixed material and let it degas for several days at temperature. The batches were small enough not to worry about homogenization.

The molten material was then poured into small molds to make a glass blank from which the lenses would be made. The newly made blank would then be annealed.

Annealing is cooling slowly from high molten temperatures to one that wouldn't fracture when the sand mold was broken open at room temperature.

Our process was crude, and we lost many test blanks due to bubbles, ream, and inclusions like stones and dirt. Some stones and dirt were in the raw flint ore, and some from the fire brick lining as it slowly disintegrated.

Each of the test batches ran large enough to make ten test blanks. It only took one hundred and fifty-seven runs to identify the right calcined flint and lead mixture for an optical-level glass.

Our first three runs of one hundred blanks yielded a twenty percent success rate. That meant we got twenty good useable blanks for every one hundred blanks made.

A failure was any blank with defects in the viewing portion of the glass. Small defects near the edges were permissible. Only the central portion, about half the diameter of the blank, had to be near perfect.

That sounded terrible, but it was good enough for our needs. The failures would be examined, and if they were rejected for bubbles and ream, they would be recycled back into our molten glass.

Those with dirt and stones in the center of the blank would end up on the save for possible future use pile. After all, they could be leaded or embedded in concrete to make windows that would admit light but not air.

We were in business now that we had glass blanks that could be polished. A small water wheel powered our polishing pad. The pad itself was made from sheep skin with fine sand embedded. There was a series of pads with ever finer sands.

The ideal grit would be diamond dust, but that wasn't available, so we were limited to the clarity of the final product. It was good enough for our purposes.

Each reading stone was ground and polished until its geometry met our requirements.

It cost us about a silver, a finished reading stone. Sales and distribution were adding another silver to the process. We would sell them for ten silvers per stone, making a decent profit.

My business arrangement with the glassmaker was fifty-fifty. Plus, I got to tax his profit! I kept taxes at five percent on the profit of manufactured items to encourage production. At the same time, there would be a tradition of taxation to support the Barony.

Another glass issue to be addressed was the making of flat glass. The glassblower would lay a molten glass gathering on a tightly held bed of sand. A heavy metal roller would then form a flat sheet of glass.

This glass was equivalent to the glass windows found in colonial American homes. The cut panes were full of inclusions, dirt and stones, bubbles, and ream. The ream was distortion, introduced by the poorly homogenized glass, leaving visible flow paths.

This glass in modern America was called greenhouse quality. It lets light through.

Chapter 7

The eyeglasses wouldn't be a technical problem. They would be a distribution issue since people had two eyes, which weren't always the same regarding vision.

That meant we had to test people's vision. We would have to open optometry shops. Then we would need trained people to staff them.

The optometrist would use a Tumbling E chart since some patients would be mute or illiterate. I was glad I had seen that chart in the book on eyeglasses. The Tumbling E chart would be used on all patients rather than have to work with two different types and avoid thoughts of favoritism.

The letter E would be shown as facing left, right, up, and down, or if it was repeated. All the patients would have to do was point their hand in which direction the E was facing.

As the lines descended, the E would be smaller. There would be a maximum of six Es for the smaller lines.

Once fitted, the eyeglasses would be similar to those I was used to. We skipped over the original *pince-nez* and ribbon-held glasses. There would be arms to extend over the ears.

The only technical issue was making screws small enough to allow folding arms. The Smith's apprentice assigned the project solved it using a small rivet.

The frame itself would be made from casein plastic. I had Agnes and Father Timothy present when I taught a dairymaid how to make milk-based plastic. The good Father needed to see that it was science rather than witchcraft, and the nurse needed to see the possibilities.

I heated one cup of milk about as hot as hot chocolate. I added it to a bowl with four teaspoons of vinegar.

When the milk started curdling, I used a slotted spoon to lift the curds out. I placed the curds on a thick cloth and then pressed the cloth on them to get as much liquid out as possible.

I then kneaded the curds until they were one mass. I then pressed this mass into molds, forming the right and left arms for the eyeglasses.

We let them sit for two days. After the plastic had cured, shrinking a little, I popped them out of the mold.

Thumping them on the table showed how durable they would be.

"Future arms will have iron hinges impressed before the plastic cures."

Agnes was the most excited.

"Do you realize that we could mass produce buttons? We need to drill holes in a bone disk to make a button. This method would be much faster. Can you add any dye to it?"

"Yes, we only have one material shortage to overcome."

Father Timothy fell right into it.

"We need more milk cows."

Lady Agnes asked, "Where can we get those?"

I explained, "The first thing is to send runners out to all the surrounding Baronies and inquire if anyone has cows for sale."

I continued, "Next, we will see if any can be shipped in from other ports."

Father Timothy asked, "Would goat milk work?"

"Any milk would work, even from mice, though they may be hard to milk."

The others didn't know if I was joking, but my grin gave it away. With a very serious look, I declared Father Timothy could be our mouse herder.

That did it. Laughter was the order of the day. Even poor put upon Father Timothy joined in.

"Seriously, any milk would work, but cow's milk is the only one that would be plentiful enough."

I pretended to have another thought and rubbed my chin before saying.

"Unless we could get some elephants. No, on second thought, Father Timothy's mice would scare the elephants away."

The milkmaid was giggling so hard I thought she would wet herself.

Agnes huffed. "I see that we have naught else to do here."

She turned and walked away.

Father Timothy called after her, "My mice could make you some buttons."

We collapsed in laughter once more.

It didn't take long for the tale of Father Timothy's mice to make the rounds. Mice started showing up in the tithing bowl.

It was hard to tell if they got the joke or thought it was serious. At least no one came up with an elephant.

Eyeglasses would cost one hundred silver a pair or one gold. We would have twenty silver manufacturing costs for the eyeglasses and carrying case and maybe another twenty in sales and distribution.

These would remain a prestige item for some time to come.

When sales started to decline, we could lower the price while working to lower manufacturing costs.

I saw no problem selling a hundred pairs in London for ten thousand silver and a net profit of six thousand. That would go a long way towards our budget needs for the next several years.

While more cows were being sought, I pondered on making a brass spyglass, a small hand-held telescope used on horseback or a ship's deck.

It would have three lenses and about six times magnification. If collapsed, the scope would be five and a half inches folded and sixteen inches extended. There would be a sun hood that extended to cut down on glare. The hood was included in the length.

Getting the focal length correct would be the trick. Even though I had read formulas, I struggled to wrap my head around infinite and horizon focal points.

We will take the easy way to focus, sliding the tubes back and forth like turning the knob on binoculars. Brass would be used because of the elements, especially salt water. The third lens would be an inverter lens, as the image would be upside down without it.

These scopes wouldn't be cheap to make. My rough guess was four hundred silvers in total. The asking price would be fifteen hundred silver or fifteen gold. Not cheap by any long shot, but if a ship's Captain could see pirates a long way away or a field scout could see the enemy, they would be priceless.

Hmm, maybe we could express that priceless thought in our advertising. I knew there was a newspaper in ancient Rome but didn't know if any were available in London.

To my knowledge, the paper would have to be handwritten, so many wouldn't be available.

I knew Abbott Luke was sending copies of our newspaper to London. He was also sending letters to the various Monasteries around the country, telling them about the printing press he had.

Setting the optical instruments aside, I saw Tom Smith the next day.

He sent a message for me to stop by at my convenience. As I strolled out of the Keep to his in-town facility, I hoped it wasn't another ambush for improvements.

It wasn't. Tom was proud to show me that he and his men had made a screw for his large metal lathe to cut to the nearest one-thousandth inch.

I was jubilant. This development meant we could implement mass production.

Not that it would start tomorrow, but mass production could start by early winter. The first production line would be for crossbows and bolts.

It was as true now as it was in the future. Military needs forced advancements.

"Tom, you must make jigs, fixtures, and go-no-go gauges to manufacture crossbows. The lathe and gauge blocks are to be kept under lock and key. Only the secondary devices will be at the manufacturing site."

I continued, well, almost continued. I had been about to say this was as big a secret as the Manhattan Project. But it is better not to open that can of worms.

"This advancement should be kept secret from most of our people. Only those with a need to know are to be aware of gauge blocks and the lathe. You must set up a special room to store and work with them."

I had used the term need to know several times before, so it was understood what I meant.

"Aye, I understand, My Lord. This method will change a lot of things. We want to keep our competitive advantage."

I hadn't introduced the word technology or its context. Maybe it was time.

I arranged for a meeting at Owen-nap's Keep in three days. That allowed a message to be sent to John Chandler and have him come from Saltash.

Three days later, I sat in our meeting room at the Keep with Eleanor, Tom Smith, Father Timothy, Abbott Luke, and

Bartholomew Miller. Bartholomew, or Bart, was the head of the crossbow manufacturing process.

Thad was there to take notes, and as usual, Sara Farmer provided security outside the room. Without being told anything, Linda Runner had magically shown up to run errands as needed. She sat outside the door waiting for a summons.

As people arrived, I watched Thad sharpen a quill to take notes. It occurred to me that we could now make steel nibs for pens. If we had rubber, we could make fountain pens. Every Monk in the world would bless my name.

Something else occurred.

"Thad, where do you keep our meeting notes?"

"In a box in my room, My Lord."

I had given up on him using my name.

"We need to come up with a better method of storing them. Someone could steal them."

Tom Smith said, "We could build a metal safe into the wall of our secure map room. Guards are always outside the one door. Someone would have to take the whole Keep to access them."

"Make it so."

Thad got a panicked look.

"I have to reference my notes frequently. That is why I keep them close by."

"You won't have to store all your notes there, just those from meetings like this."

"How can I tell which ones go where?"

"I will tell you which ones will be put in a folder marked 'Secret'. The folder will have the names of people allowed to read the notes. This method is called compartmentalization.

"Not everyone given a secret clearance will be allowed to read everything marked secret.

"To read any folder, the person must go to the secure room. They will have to surrender all containers before entering or showing their contents. No writing materials will be allowed in with them, and they will be searched on the way out. Thad, you must be present when a person is in that room."

"These rules apply to everyone, including Eleanor and myself."

By including my wife and me, no one could claim privilege.

"No one will ever learn our secrets," boasted Father Timothy.

"They will. It will just take them longer with these precautions."

I had to approve security procedures during the cold war. No matter what we did, the Soviets would eventually break them.

When all were present, I explained we could start mass production and keep the base knowledge secret by only allowing jigs, fixtures, and go-no-go gauges in the factory.

I explained that workstations would be in a row. Only one part would be made at each station. Since the parts were cold forged, they would be close to the correct size.

The part would then be placed in a fixture. Anything preventing the part from fitting would be sanded or filed off. Parts that had gaps from the fixture wall would be rejected and remelted.

Many parts of the same dimension could be made quickly. If a part proved too difficult, we would set up multiple stations to even out the production rate of parts.

These parts would be put in bins available at assembly workstations. Again, one part only at a station unless it was a subassembly.

It took hours to work out the details, and we had to send Linda Runner to order luncheon for us.

It ended with Bart agreeing to provide one of each part to Tom so an apprentice could make the appropriate tool.

We converted one of the guest longhouses for our new factory. Someone said a perfect assembly line is ten feet wide and a mile long. While we couldn't accomplish it in fact, we did it in principle.

Chapter 8

Eleanor was getting a little cranky, being in her seventh month of pregnancy. She told me it was her seventh year. All I could do was agree that it had been a long time, but she was almost finished.

That was when she threatened to finish me. I decided that I had urgent business elsewhere. Anywhere else.

While I was having an ale with John Steward in a small room off the kitchen, I thought about the coming birth of our child.

While mortality rates were down, a frequent problem in childbirth was eye infections. While the main cause was a sexual disease, any infection could leave a child blind.

Silver nitrate was used to prevent infection. We hadn't developed this chemical yet. We hadn't developed any new chemicals yet. Most trades, from leather to printing, used some form of a chemical, but I hadn't led the development of true chemistry.

The making of bases and acids was the foundation of chemical processing.

The first step in my new chemistry lab was to make a still. It would be a primitive distilling apparatus like the alembic still created by an Arab.

It had three parts: a still pot or crucible and a head at the top of the pot to allow gases to collect and cool. The cooled liquid would flow down a tube into a receiving container.

I intended to start with hydrochloric acid, a basic building block for many chemicals. I selected one of the bright young Monks to become the first chemist.

It was fortunate for us that the Church encouraged the brightest to become Monks. The young men were taught to read, write and work with numbers.

Thus the Monastery was my recruiting ground. It is a shame that convents didn't train young women. The convents were more like storage facilities for inconvenient women who couldn't be killed.

It wasn't that many of the women weren't bright. It just wasn't a selection criterion. Since there were no convents in the area other than a small one in Saltash, it wasn't a consideration.

As our students graduated, the best would be put to work on our projects. Even the worse students would benefit from an education.

The new chemist and I went to the glassblowers, where I explained what was needed. They were to build ten of the glass stills. Production and possible breakage were the reasons for more than one.

A shed a considerable walking distance from the Keep and village was to be the chemistry lab. Who knew what mistakes would be made? The shed was next to a small stream.

Wooden benches were installed, and a small water tower was set up. A hand pump operated by the chemist would fill the water tower.

The most important device was a fume hood. Using the venturi method, we pumped the fumes up a ten-foot-tall flue for safe dispersion.

Solid waste would be put into clay-lined barrels and taken to Saltash to be dumped at sea. Not environmentally friendly, but not in our backyard.

A pit was dug away from the water supply, and an outhouse was built over it. An extension was built onto the lab so the Monk, Peter Owen-nap, could sleep over if needed or have a comfortable place to wait out a rainstorm.

Peter was an orphan foundling. That was why his last name was Owen-nap. I even wondered if he was a half-brother of the real Baron Owen-nap.

His looks argued against that. He had wild hair and bushy eyebrows. The perfect mad scientist look. He would also be eligible for one of the first pairs of eyeglasses we made.

No matter his looks, he was as smart as a whip. I explained basic laboratory safety to him and why it was needed. He seemed to get it and had no desire to kill himself.

His first project would be to distill water, as pure water was necessary for many compounds.

While the stills were being made, I commissioned John Chandler to buy Epsom Salts and ammonium chloride, known as sal ammoniac in London, by the hundredweight.

Tom Smith was to make funnels about the same size as a five-gallon can. A metal plate would be placed over a coal fire.

Epsom Salts and ammonium chloride would be ground in a small hand-turned ball mill. I was lucky. Tom had made a ball mill before for one of the grain mill operators who wanted to produce a better grade of flour.

Unfortunately, the miller died before the ball mill could be used, so it sat in Tom's storage area. He was glad to sell it to me at a reduced price. I think he hosed me.

He was getting to be a good enough friend that I wrote it off as a joke. Paybacks are hell. Wait till he gets his tax bill. That would be no joke!

The finely ground Epsom Salts and ammonium chloride would be placed on the metal plate, and the funnel inverted over it.

When the plate was heated, the mixture gave off gaseous hydrogen chloride and ammonia. The ammonia would sublimate on the funnel sides and the gas flow to the top of the funnel where it would be redirected through a tube into distilled water.

The gas would rapidly combine with the water to yield hydrochloric acid. Once no more gas was produced, we would boil the acid to drive off any water not combined, leaving concentrated hydrochloric acid.

This setup was to be a proof of concept before it was scaled up to commercial quantities. At least commercial quantities for this day and age.

A by-product of our cement manufacturing process was sulfur dioxide created when we roasted the lime. Peter used the upside down funnel to capture the gas. The gas was then discharged into a lead-lined barrel.

Moist air was pumped into the chamber, and when the two combined, liquid sulfuric acid was formed at the bottom of the barrel.

Again, we had proof of concept.

We had to build a device to capture the fumes from the lime roasting process. Using a by-product was a strong argument for spending money to reduce incomplete combustion.

We didn't want the impurities generated from poorly burnt coal.

The simplest and most used preparation of nitric acid that I remember is by adding concentrated sulfuric acid to potassium nitrate, also known as saltpeter. This mixture is heated to melt the pasty mixture and distill the nitric acid.

I was pushing the ability to make silver nitrate because of the dangers of conjunctivitis to a newborn.

I had been very linear in the process of development. First is hydrochloric acid, to make sulfuric acid, sulfuric acid to manufacture nitric acid, and silver nitrate.

When I started investigating silver nitrate by bringing the books on the subject to my eidetic brain, I found the dangers outweighed the benefits. We had no syphilis or other venereal diseases in our immediate area.

If there were, Agnes would have been all over them. Every sailor wanting to come ashore in Saltash required a short arm inspection, as we called it in the army. We had the cleanest whores in the world.

Common cleanliness practices and checking the eyes of everyone before coming near the child would reduce the risks below that of applying silver nitrate. These precautions would only be in place for the first week of life.

It was not a wasted effort because we now could make the best mirrors in the world.

We needed saltpeter and sulfuric acid. We now knew how to produce the acid. I went to the stables looking for a source of saltpeter.

I ended up finding two sources. The most obvious was the bottom of the waste pile. This pile of straw and horse droppings was removed from the stalls and placed in a heap behind the stables.

I had never given it a thought. Just like nightsoil, this stuff shouldn't be kept here. That would have to change, but it was a blessing right now.

I had two stable hands dig to the bottom of the pile with pitchforks. Not for the Lord to do such work! Besides, it stinks.

As they reached the bottom of the pile, they started to turn over the crystalized saltpeter. Pay dirt!

I promised them a bonus of twelve silver if they would turn over the whole pile and collect the crystals in a clean clay pot.

They eagerly accepted the tasks.

One of the lads commented this would be easier if the sand hadn't stuck to some of the crystals?"

I asked, "What sand?"

"The sands in each stall. The stablemaster claims it is easier on their hooves."

I didn't doubt that, but I had to check out the stables.

"Come with me, boys."

These boys were older than me, but some speech habits were hard to break.

I had them dig down in the sand in an empty but well-used stall. They only went about six inches and hit the mother lode. The horse's urine had been settling there for years.

They had periodically replaced the top four inches of sand but had never dug down that deep. There were enough saltpeter crystals to prototype and handle the first production run.

And yes, I thought of gunpowder.

Forming nitric acid in our prototyping was the easiest step yet. Dissolve the saltpeter with sulfuric acid and voila, we had nitric acid.

We combined ammonia (a by-product from our hydrochloric acid production) with sodium hydroxide to make a silver nitrate solution. The sodium hydroxide was merely salt dissolved in distilled water, yielding a yellowish solution.

We then gently lowered a bit of refined silver. In this case, a melted silver coin with the dross skimmed off the top.

The acid solution was heated until the silver started to bubble. Then we let the solution stand until it completely evaporated.

 The next step was to mix sodium hydroxide (evaporated salt water) equal to the silver nitrate. Then add distilled water until the mixture dissolves.

A black precipitate forms, ammonia is added until the precipitate completely dissolves. Add a small amount of sugar and stir until its dissolution.

Pour the solution into a tray and place the glass in the tray so only one side is in contact with the solution.

We then heated the tray. We had to do this within two hours, or our solution would decay into a deadly poison.

The tray with the glass in it was heated just enough to cause a reaction.

By trial and error, we found the best heat time combination. For us, it was just below boiling and leaving in for an hour.

When removed, the glass had a true mirrored surface.

All the steps above sound easy. They were easy compared to the chemists who discovered the reactions in the future. I had the cheat of an eidetic memory.

It still took several months and all of Peter's eyebrows to accomplish all this.

At the end of it, I was salivating at the potential silvers. That is until we silver our first glass.

At that time, we produced flat glass by blowing a bubble and then rolling it flat on a bed of sand. To say the optical quality was poor was an understatement.

However, Eleanor and her maids, Anne and Marion, were impressed with the first mirror. Peter and I made up three mirrors with plastic frames for them.

Once more, I was reminded that we needed more cows!

The ladies were playing with their mirrors in front of Sara Farmer when she realized they could be used to safely look around corners.

All of a sudden, the need for mirrors went up. Of course, every woman and most men wanted one when they were seen in public.

Maybe Tom Smith or Mark Woodson could devise a frame to protect the glass edges of wood or metal.

Chapter 9

I had to spend much time reorganizing all the Baronies into Districts. The district's residents still considered themselves Baronies, but from an administrative view, it was better to have a central government.

Then, there was the judging of crimes. I was the last resort in crimes leading to execution. Each Knight in the District could sentence someone to the work crews, most commonly road crews.

We didn't spend much effort preventing the criminals from fleeing the work crews. Our population was small enough that they couldn't blend in. They had to go outside my area and become someone else's problem.

Not nice, but I wasn't about to build or support a prison system.

The occasional murder was another thing. I was harsh. The murders in our area were crimes of passion rather than profit. I had them all hanged. One was for profit. A man killed his parents to inherit their farm. He inherited a noose.

One of my projects was to create a banking system. Unlike before I came along, the economy was booming. The silvers were flowing from my treasury to people's pockets.

Some had silver they couldn't spend immediately. This newly rich included Tom Smith and the other tradesmen. For them, a bank would be a place to keep their coins safe.

They would also draw a low interest rate, so their money was making money. The longer they commit to leaving it, the higher the interest rate.

The bank would use these long-term investments to make loans, but the idea was to put more money into circulation. I wanted to encourage business ventures and farmers to purchase their farms.

These loans were secure because borrowers were working with real property. Mark Woodson was the head of the bank's loan committee, and it was tough. There would be no bank failures on his watch.

I didn't explain how commercial banks got in trouble in my time by investing in the stock market or encouraging risky loans.

In the long run, we would benefit from these loans. I allowed the bank to loan twice as much money as they had on deposit. This policy increased the money flow and growth.

Since we didn't have fiat money, the only way it could work was to keep all records on paper. The actual silver would circulate fast.

A farmer would borrow money to buy his farm. The bank would make the loan. The closing would be at the bank. The farmer would be handed the silver and then turn around and return it to my account as I sold them the farm.

Thus, the bank always had silver to loan, and the farmer was now a tax-paying citizen. We could only get in trouble if I spent silver outside the Barony. Otherwise, it just flowed in a circle.

The money flowed around that circle so fast (up time called velocity) that no one knew how much silver was in the system.

Even so, I needed a source of more silver to offset money outside of the Barony and increase the money supply so we could build faster.

Things were humming.

Nothing happened overnight.

Another project I started with Tom and Andrew Glassman was making a better grade of flat glass for windows and mirrors.

Our technology wasn't up to the float glass made in the twenty-first century by drawing hot glass over a molten bed of lead.

What we could do was the 'drawn glass' method. This method lowered a steel bar on chains into a molten glass furnace. The molten glass would adhere to the steel bar.

The bar would be raised slowly with the glass pulling like taffy. The glass would pass through a series of steel rollers polished to a mirror finish. They would keep thinning the glass until we had the desired thickness.

We planned two-tenths of an inch thick for window glass and plate glass one-half inch thick.

There were two technical issues to be addressed. Heating a hot furnace to melt the glass and a mirror finish on the steel rollers.

Using compressed air could create a fire as hot as the blast furnace. But we would need a brick tough enough to withstand the heat.

With a blast furnace, we weren't concerned about small amounts of dirt or stone in the steel batch. Glass was a different story. We needed brick that wouldn't decay rapidly.

After bringing up a book on types of clays, I realized we had the clay we needed. Fire clay was found at the bottom of coal seams. Those we had in plenty.

Eleanor was rude enough to interrupt all these ventures by presenting me with the most beautiful daughter in the world.

I wasn't allowed near Eleanor when she was giving birth. That was women's work. But I didn't have to be in the room to hear what she thought of men, particularly me, as she went through her labor.

The entire Keep knew her feelings on the matter.

Agnes informed me Eleanor was fortunate in having a large birth canal and exit. She didn't have to cut, lessening the chances of infection.

I was forgiven when I saw our new daughter in her arms.

This birth was my first child in either period, so I could excuse myself for being biased. Okay, I was like most first-time fathers, proud as all get out.

We named her Catherine Elizabeth Saltash Owen-nap. Eleanor's mother was Catherine, mine Elizabeth, and then our Baronies.

When she was a week old, I joked, "The suitors will be showing up any day now."

Eleanor replied, "Not until she is two, and she has a good chance of surviving."

I forgot the risks young children face.

With Agnes, our resident clean freak, watching over things, there was a low risk of infection. Not only was the nursery scrubbed regularly, but anyone coming near the baby, much less in contact, had to bathe and wear clean clothes.

Agnes decided what constituted a bath and checked our clothes.

I returned to change doublets one day because I hadn't noticed a food spill. I praised Agnes for her vigilance.

If you had a cough or a visible rash, there was no way you were getting near our daughter.

She was appointed her guard at birth and would be with her most of her life. The guard, Janet Farmer, was sixteen but was deadly at hand-to-hand, sword, spear, and crossbow.

She is a pleasant person until aroused. Then hell won't hold her back. The dark-complected girl was tall for her age. Her head of hair was as black as midnight. A ready smile and a lovely soprano voice made her easy to have around.

Johanna Farmer was to be Cathy's nurse. Johanna, a female version of John, is short, only four and a half feet tall, but built like a tank. She could have played one of Tolkien's dwarves if she had a beard. I think she shaved.

Her voice was grating, but she could sing lullabies like an angel. She looked more the norm for our area, with brown hair and eyes to match.

I understood the last name being Farmer for so many people. It was the main occupation until recently. Father Timothy explained that most people were named after the apostles. Janet for James, and Johanna for John.

That explained why so many names were repeated. It was convenient that Eleanor's mother's name was Catherine, and her new stepmother was also Catherine.

When I asked about Eleanor's name, I learned Eleanor is a version of Helen, and

Helen was the mother of
Emperor Constantine the Great.

The first Constantine, the Christian
Emperor, had been acclaimed imperator by
his troops at Eboracum, which became
York, England.

Needless to say, that family was revered in
England. I wondered what the reaction
would be if I ever had to conquer
Constantinople.

The former Baron Saltash, who I still refer
to as Baron in public and William in private,
was in Owen-nap within three days of
Cathy's birth. My wife, father-in-law,
stepmother-in-law, Father Timothy, and
others rebuked me for the nickname of
Cathy.

I yielded in public, but she was my
wonderful Cathy in private. Her guard and
nurse were on my side.

If possible, William was prouder of his
granddaughter than I was.

His wife Catherine was like all women of all
time. She held the baby when she could and
cooed at it.

Cathy seemed to be a happy child, smiling
all the time. Eleanor told me this was gas. I
didn't buy it.

I did become a hero to all the women in my
extended Barony and even some of the men
when I invented the safety pin. All it took

was a simple drawing, and Tom had three apprentices doing nothing but making the pins.

I was inspired to invent the pins when I saw them wrap Cathy up in several layers of cloth. One extra good thing came out of it. The new safety pins were a novelty that I couldn't change a diaper. The women argued about whose turn it was. Poor me.

Being a hero once to the women wasn't enough. I told Agnes how women could express their milk, store it in an icebox, and then heat it for later to be spoon-fed.

While a hero to women, men who had to get up in the middle of the night to feed the baby weren't singing my praises.

Again, I was fortunate to have a nanny who could perform that duty. Mark Woodson, whose wife gave birth simultaneously with Eleanor, probably wouldn't send me a Christmas card.

It was no big loss since Christmas cards hadn't been established yet. Mark made a point in every meeting about being woken in the middle of the night to feed his son.

I thought that woman was subservient to the man in this day and age. Apparently not.

Fatherhood was a pleasure. I got to hold my baby and then hand her off if she smelled or cried too much. I didn't mind getting up and walking her in the middle of the night if she was awake and had a tummy ache from gas.

I would walk and pat her on the back until she let out an enormous burp. I didn't know babies could be that loud.

During the day, I spent time on the new banking system. There would be a branch office in each District. We had a poured concrete building put up in the village.

A basement was dug out to contain the safe room. We didn't have safes as such. Our safe was a room that took up half the basement. At night, the door to the safe room was bolted shut. Two guards spent the night outside the safe room with a heavily locked door at the bottom of the basement steps.

The guards were disabled soldiers but could handle the counterweighted heavy bar. There were six guards on a rotating basis.

The guards kept a logbook of all traffic in the safe room. All silver, copper, and gold were stored here after hours, plus the bank's ledgers.

If we had a warning of an attack, the contents of the saferoom would be moved to the Keep's saferoom. If not, the guards locked in had enough food and water for a month. After that, they had orders to surrender.

A loan committee of five prominent citizens would decide what loans to make. Between them, they knew almost everyone in the district. The same setup would be at every branch office.

Chapter 10

Since I was getting more sleep than several men of my acquaintance, I started a new project.

This project also involved chemistry, but I put another young monk in charge. Peter Owen-nap had enough on his plate. A harsh fact was that the manufacture of gunpowder might blow up the young monk on the project, and Peter had become too valuable to risk.

Jude Glassman was a young orphan picked up by the Monks and trained at the Monastery. His mother had died in childbirth.

His father, a glassblower by trade, coughed at the wrong moment when trying to blow glass and sucked boiling air into his lungs. He died within a week, leaving Jude an orphan.

He was a quiet young man who followed instructions to the letter but wasn't given to try things on his own. A trait needed for this job.

He had a slight build, brown hair, and eyes. A cheerful disposition like all the Monks who came from the Monastery. Maybe that was indicative of life there. The boys certainly had a lot more freedom working for me.

Their pay rate was such that all the girls eyed them. If Peter had eyebrows, I think he would have been married. They would grow back, and I would have to build a cottage near his chemistry lab for him and his new wife.

I was correct in my thoughts about Peter. A young lady knew that eyebrows grew back and found herself with a child. When he told me he wanted to marry her, I laughed and told him to post the banns. I would provide the newlyweds with a cottage.

Before the wedding, I gave them a lecture about safety in the lab. I wanted his new spouse to understand how dangerous his work could be.

I'm certain she would help him keep his head screwed on tight. He was a married man now with responsibilities. No more losing eyebrows. Three times was enough.

I gave the lecture in the lab when I realized there wasn't a shower or eyewash station. All work was suspended until they were in place. Also, buckets of sand were stationed around the room. I had been lax, but luckily, we didn't need the precautions.

Joan Farmer, his soon-to-be wife, took my lecture seriously. She took it upon herself to watch Peter as he made his mixtures. She was literate, so she took notes of each experiment performed and the results.

Her notes were more legible than Peter's had ever been, so I felt I came ahead on the deal.

It also meant a young child would learn chemistry in about five years. Now what could go wrong with that?

Making gunpowder wasn't that difficult if you had the correct materials. Mix seventy-five parts potassium nitrate, fifteen parts charcoal, and ten parts sulfur to make black powder.

The ingredients should be finely ground separately before mixing. We would use a small ball mill.

Then Peter would mix them with a small amount of distilled water to form a biscuit-dough consistency. The distilled water was to clump the powder. The original method was for the gunners to pee on the powder.

The mixture would be chilled in an icebox, then strained through a cheesecloth, and dried before being transferred to a copper container in a cool, dry area.

The final mix in the ball mill was to mill the charcoal and sulfur together for 4 hours, then add the saltpeter, and mill the mixture for another 24 hours.

The mixture would be explosive at this time and had to be handled carefully. Peter and his wife were provided with slippers to wear in the lab. No metal which could strike a spark was allowed in the lab. Windows would provide light. The bullseye glass used let light through, and that was it.

Before that could start, we needed much more potassium nitrate than we had. Making nitric acid had used up our supply.

We were going to dig up the night soil pits we had been filling. Enough time had passed for a good supply of potassium nitrate crystals. There would be enough experiments to refine the gunpowder and ensure a good mixture.

We were trying for a blasting powder grade. We hoped to make cannon-grade powder eventually. There was no way possible for us to make the best grade of 5FG. It would take better mills and sieves.

In anticipation of needing a lot more potassium nitrate in the future, we made niter beds.

My readings described niter beds were prepared by mixing manure with either mortar or wood ashes, common earth, and organic materials such as straw to give porosity to a compost pile typically 4 feet high, 6 feet wide, and 15 feet long.

The heap would be under a cover from the rain, kept moist with urine, and often turned to accelerate the decomposition. Then finally leached with water after approximately one year to remove the soluble calcium nitrate, which was then converted to potassium nitrate by filtering through potash.

We could not speed up the year needed to form the crystals. But we only needed gunpowder for mining operations now, so it wasn't a problem.

In the long run, I wanted to furnish my troops with cannons and rifles, but that was well into the future. At least, I hoped we wouldn't need them soon.

It was also time to have a conversation I had been putting off for over a year. The recent advances in chemistry and what was about to happen with gunpowder were beyond being God Touched.

I needed to tell my story to Eleanor, Father Timothy, and Abbot Luke. Eleanor because she is my wife and partner. The two holy men because if they accepted what was to come, no one else would raise questions.

John Steward already knew my story.

I chose to tell Eleanor first. After ensuring no nosey Parkers were hanging around our bed chamber, I told her.

"Dear, we have to talk."

These were the most dreaded words in a relationship when uttered seriously, and I was serious.

From the look on her face, time and distance hadn't changed the force of those words.

"There is nothing wrong I just have to tell you a few things about myself that I have kept secret."

She replied cautiously, "Oh."

"I hardly know where to begin."

"The beginning is usually a good place."

"Maybe the middle this time. I'm living a second life if you will."

"What do you mean?"

"I died and woke up in the body of Baron Owen-nap."

"When was this?"

"Do you remember the story about the late Abbott trying to kill Owen-nap?"

"I do."

She was speaking in a dead, even voice like one confronting a madman who could attack them at any minute. I would have reacted the same.

"He was unconscious, what I know as a coma. When he regained consciousness, it wasn't him anymore. It was me. He must have died, and I was placed in his body."

"Then who are you?"

"I was born in the year one thousand nine hundred and eighteen anno domini. I lived to the age of ninety-two years."

"You mean the world doesn't end in the year one thousand?"

94

It was strange that she picked that up out of my statement. I knew that bible scholars had theorized that the years leading up to one thousand were turbulent, culminating in the end of the world. I didn't realize it was discussed three hundred years before the event.

"The world continued. It was a false prophecy."

"Good, I can change my nightly prayer."

She continued, "You haven't acted mad, so continue with your story."

I explained my first life, even though I had been married for many years but had no children.

She wanted details when I got to the parts about my military career. When I described the horrors of twenty-first-century warfare, she wept.

She grew more accepting as I gave her more details of my life. When I told her that I ended up as one of my nation's forces' leaders, she told me.

"I knew you were a war leader; this explains it."

"There is more. I have a funny memory. We called it an eidetic memory. If I see a page in a scroll, I will remember the words forever. I may not understand them, but when I think of that page, I can see every word on it."

She declared, "Then you are God Touched!"

"I guess in a way I am. I never thought of it in that manner."

I continued explaining my love of engineering and how I continued my education my entire life.

Eleanor was almost blasé about trains, airplanes, and automobiles. It was the future.

I continued, "When I woke up in the Baron's body, I knew the language and something of the world around me. I had to tell John Steward about my condition, and he helped me through my first year."

"Why are you telling me this story now?"

"The two laboratories I have put up have invented some wonderful things. Father Timothy and Abbott Luke will have many questions. I must explain my circumstances to them, but I wanted to tell you first."

"Thank you. You must be here for a reason."

"If I am, I don't know what it is."

"It is said that people who are saints don't claim to be. I think you are."

Oh no, is she going worship me and keep her distance?

"Have you ever made love to a saint?"

"It appears that I have, many times."

"I'm a lusty man. That is what I am. Come here, My Lady."

She did, and the rest of the night was ours.

The next day, I noticed she and John Steward were as thick as thieves. They would talk for a while and then look over at me. When I finished my breakfast, I joined them.

"I hope you have gossiped enough."

Eleanor said, "Oh, we are just beginning. I have many questions for you, dear husband. John has shared a few things that you have told him. I need to know more, much more."

I groaned. I knew Eleanor well enough now that I might as well surrender immediately.

"Yes, dear, I will answer all in the privacy of our room."

As I said this, I looked around; people listening avidly now turned their heads.

"Until this evening, husband."

She called me husband because wives didn't use their husbands' first names publicly. She could call me, My Lord. Only hell would freeze over before that happened.

I loved my fiercely independent wife.

"I sent Abbott Luke and Father Timothy a messenger asking them to meet me at the Church. I intend to explain all to them."

Eleanor got a frightened look, "Be careful, My Lord."

She was scared for me.

I had chosen the Church as the meeting place because demons and witches couldn't cross the threshold according to local belief.

They were both there waiting. I didn't mess around.

"I need to share a story with you about an old man who died and woke up in the body of a young Baron."

The Abbott looked perplexed. Father Timothy nodded his head as though he had been waiting for this.

"Died and woke up in the body of Baron Owen-nap. I have no explanation for how this happened."

Father Timothy serenely asked, "How old were you?"

"Ninety-two."

"What year did you die?"

"The year two thousand and ten anno domini."

"How did the Church fare?"

"It was still there and active when I died."

Abbott Luke was sitting there with his mouth open, gaping like a fish.

"Father, you seem to be taking this calmly."

"I have wondered about you for some time. You have made no claims to be God Touched, but you have brought wonderous things to us beyond what any recorded God Touched has before."

He continued, "Most God Touched are weak in the head and do not live long. Many say they are simpletons. You are anything but that."

Abbott Luke finally found his voice.

"Are you a witch?"

Chapter 11

"No, I'm a man just like you, well, almost like you. I don't understand why I'm here. With my knowledge, I'm trying to do my best for these people. They are now my people, and I'm responsible for their health and well-being."

"You could still be a witch."

"Abbott, what does a witch do?"

"They make foul concoctions, curse people who offend them, and dance naked under the full moon's light. They then lay on an altar with an upside down cross for the devil and consort with him."

Eleanor didn't help when she told him, "I've eaten some of his cooking. It was a foul concoction."

So, I had her try grits. Sue me.

John Steward spoke up, "He kills people who offend him."

Thanks, guys!

Father Timothy spoke up. "Killing someone isn't the same as cursing them, plus I have seen no evidence of misuse of the cross or altar. Since they are the only ones around, he doesn't appear to be guilty of that."

Eleanor returned with, "As far as dancing naked under a full moon, I can testify he is a terrible dancer. It's hard to think of him flapping his dangly bits around like that.

Thanks once more, dear wife.

The Abbott said again, "I don't think he is a witch. I wondered about all the knowledge you bring to us, Owen-nap. It seems more than any mortal should know."

"You are correct in thinking that way. I have what is called an eidetic memory. When I see or hear something, I remember it forever. Not that I necessarily understand it."

I went on, "Once I see a page in a book, I can think what is on that page with perfect clarity. I may not understand the meaning of the words, but I can read them in my mind over and over.

"If the thought presented is not too complex, I can usually figure out what is meant. That is how I can dictate the books and stories to my scribe. I didn't write them. I'm just repeating what I have seen or read."

"Then you must have read a lot of books. How many did they have in your time?"

"Millions."

He gasped a little. "Millions."

"The printing press you are using was invented four hundred years before I was born. There were a lot of improvements.

Also, the world's population was much larger than it is now."

"Is the Church of Rome still all-powerful?"

"It is one of the largest religions in the world but has little influence on the rulers of the world."

"How can this be?"

"The Church in my past became corrupt many years from now. There was fighting for power within the Church, resulting in the loss of respect and power for the Church."

"Is the Church still a leader in finding and preserving the world's knowledge?"

"Much of the world's knowledge is found by scientists working for governments, universities, and private companies."

Eleanor asked, "What is a university?"

"A collection of schools that teach and perform scientific research. Their teachings are more advanced than our schools. I would like to see a university system in our future."

"How is all that knowledge shared with the common people?"

"Every town and village has a library."

Father Timothy asked, "Like the great library of Alexander?"

"Yes, but each contains more tomes than that great library."

"Then everyone reads and speaks Latin."

"Only Priests of the Church. In my time, it is considered a dead language. No one writes books or papers in Latin. English, like ours, is the dominant language of learning."

Abbott Luke said, "Latin a dead language?"

"Not actually dead, static, and unchanging is a better description. No new words are added since it isn't in common use."

From there, we spent the next two days discussing the wonders of my world.

I emphasized chemistry advancements in my descriptions, both in medicine and warfare. These advancements were why I had elected to inform them of my past, present, future, or whatever.

I even told them about place names being the same but in different locations. Abbott Luke and Father Timothy thought that maybe God had decided that man was on the wrong path and had sent me back to change that path.

I didn't agree or disagree with them. It was a possibility, but I had no way of knowing.

After several days of intense questioning by the Abbott and Father Timothy, they concluded that I wasn't a witch and had a tremendous store of knowledge I could share.

They weren't certain if my being here was by divine providence but couldn't imagine any other answer. If it was the answer, then who were they to question God's action? As far as the devil, I had done too much good already to be one of his.

Before making my big reveal to the Abbott and Priest, I had worked with Peter Owen-nap to set up a series of chemical demonstrations.

Since many chemical reactions took time and some had to sit for several hours or days, we made solutions in the various stages to be shown relatively quickly. That is in the course of a day.

I explained that we needed several types of acid to produce what I would show them at the end of the day.

Eleanor and John Steward hadn't seen these processes, so they accompanied the Abbott and good Father to see what was being done.

We took them through making hydrochloric acid, which was needed to produce sulfuric acid. We had examples of all the ores and minerals used, plus how they were obtained.

From sulfuric acid, we made nitric acid. I think the idea of distillation and the capturing of gases was what impressed them most.

Abbott Luke proved to be astute.

He asked, "What if you distilled wine?"

"You would end up with a purer form of alcohol, which makes men drunk."

Looking sidewise at Eleanor, I added, "It has been known to make women drunk."

She and her maids had overindulged several days before while reading one of the romances I had dictated. It was steamy. They thought the Scottish Knight was hot.

I had to be careful which one I chose because some involved time travel.

They were all eyes when we reached the stage where a silver coin was melted. The dissolving it in nitric acid was almost sacrilegious.

A piece of glass had been chosen for its clarity and freedom of defects. I placed it in the silver nitrate solution and told them it had to be heated for several hours, but I could show them the end product.

While this was going on, Peter demonstrated making plastic from milk. Again, samples of the finished product were available so they could quickly see the end result.

Eleanor and John had caught on to what we were doing.

I told the Priest and the Abbott what the finished product would be. At that, I moved a cloth covering a beautiful, almost perfect mirror.

To put it mildly, they were impressed. They were even more impressed when I explained the economics of selling them. It was the last I ever heard of witchcraft, at least from them.

After that, we walked over to Jude Glassman's lab to show what was happening there. He hadn't burnt his eyebrows off, so he looked okay.

When we got there, two young ladies were glaring at each other. I don't think it will be long before he is married.

Before I would let anyone into the lab, they had to divest themselves of anything containing metal. John Steward proved to be a walking armory. They all had to remove their shoes and wear slippers because of metal nails.

While far from what we needed, we had a black powder that would burn fast enough to launch a small ball from a jury-rigged pipe.

Jude was able to hit a target five feet away. It wasn't very impressive as our little cannonball bounced. I explained that it was the early days of getting the right mixture. When we had it, we could shoot a nine-pound cannon ball half a mile and damage the walls of our compound.

The first good powder we made would be used for mining. We could drill holes in the seam and fill them with powder. When burned, the powder would expand gases so quickly it would remove a significant portion of the materials. What normally took days with a pick and shovel could be done in several hours.

We returned to the Keep to discuss the future. I described what we worked on with reading stones, eyeglasses, and telescopes.

Father Timothy said, "James, you will make a fortune."

"That I will, and I will reinvest that fortune to make new products to improve our people's lot in life."

The Abbott spoke grimly. "You will also have many jealous enemies who want what you have. The emperor himself may send his armies."

"That is why we are working on gunpowder. Other weapons can shoot metal balls. These can be hand-held by our troops.

"If needed, we can create the most powerful army in the world."

Everyone sat silently after that statement, thinking about the good and bad possibilities. We adjourned our meeting but agreed to meet regularly to decide how to let our people know that what was going on had the sanction of the Church.

At least the local Church, there would be no letters to the Bishops or Pope. Both Abbott and Priest recognized their superiors were secular men and would try to seize an advantage.

A messenger arrived from an exploring party in Mt. Brunwenely two days later. A bed of lead ore with a high silver content had been found at the mountain's base. He gave me a dark grey stone with a metallic shine to it. Nothing like anthracite coal.

If this were a significant find, it would change many things. Making improvements possible in an accelerated time frame.

Eleanor and I set out with our entourage of fifty to see the lead/silver ore bed the following week. These days, I went nowhere without guards.

It took a week to get everyone together and establish a supply train. Logistics were becoming a large issue in everything we did.

It took three easy days to reach the discovery. Though I was anxious to see what had been found, there was no reason to hurry.

When we arrived, I was welcomed with the good news that the ore bed appeared large. It had been exposed to heavy rains.

I had Thad make a note that we had to ensure that water could be diverted around this area. We didn't want to lose it all to another flood.

The exploration crew was as anxious as I was to know the extent of the ore bed. The explorers had cleared the entire working face and started digging around the bed.

They kept digging farther out from the center of the exposed bed. It appeared to be over a hundred yards in every direction. It would be a large open pit mine.

To say I was excited was an understatement. I arranged for half the guards to remain with the find.

The explorers were to continue with their survey of the area. They needed to find a stream that could be diverted to provide a plentiful water supply yet not put us at risk of more flooding.

Any other minerals found would be considered a bonus but not their priority.

John Steward was to establish a fort to protect the area. I was certain that once others knew what was happening here, they would try to take it from us.

It was imperative to learn more about the capabilities of Looe, Padstow, Liskeard, and Hilston.

We were now in what the Chinese had called 'interesting times.'

Chapter 12

There were many things to do to get the mining site ready to be worked. I had Thad draft a note to the road surveying crew to start locating the best route to this site.

I wanted this to be an all-weather road, so it had to be concrete. That meant we needed to find a nearby source of limestone and build a kiln.

The limestone was everywhere, so that was easy. Finding a spot wasn't. After considering the various possibilities, James Stone told me the best option would depend on where I wanted to refine the ore.

After discussions with my advisors, we decided to refine the ore near the Keep. If we refined it on the mountain, bandits could steal the silver. Shipping ore would lower the value of each shipment making it less attractive to thieves.

Notice I called them bandits and thieves. I'm sure none of my fellow Barons in the area would try to steal my silver. Right?

Refining at Owen-nap prevented the mining crew from stealing silver or lead ingots. I hated to think they would, but we were dealing with humans. This raised the concern of how to track the silver and lead at Owen-nap.

So, the only infrastructure needed at the mine was living quarters for the miners, a safe water source, and a loading dock for the wagons.

Based on that, extending the road from Bodmin would be easier.

The hardest part was finding a site for the miner's huts. Even though it was in the foothills before the mountain, there wasn't much level ground available for a compound.

For the miner's safety, the compound would have to be walled. It was decided to combine the guard's barracks with the compound. We were building another Keep.

I referred to them as huts, but they were built for winter on the mountain. A dining hall was needed to accommodate the twenty miners working the open pit.

They would be divided into five four-man crews and work from daybreak to nightfall and on weekends. They would be six-hour shifts for the most part, but still hard days.

Jim Stone recommended one of his assistants to be the supervisor in charge of the mine. Simon Miner looked like he was one of Tolkien's dwarves. Short and powerful looking.

Abbott Luke reluctantly gave up a young Monk to be the bookkeeper at the mine. I had gone to that well too many times.

The problem of not enough Monks would be settled in the coming year. The first graduates of our high school would be looking for jobs.

It would take several months to have a gravel road up to the mine, and it would be next year before a concrete road was in place.

So the process started at a slow pace. The pace of the oxen pulling wagons on a rough road. What would be a one-day trip next year was two days this year.

That meant we had to build a nightly stopping place. It had to be near water and be staffed with guards, which meant barracks and places for the wagon drivers. Luckily there was plenty of wood in the area.

That helped with the problem of buildings in the mining area and bulks of wood to shore up the road down into the pit. It never seemed to end.

Next year we plan to put up a sawmill at the mountain's base. This year all the building and support planks will be shipped in.

Back at Owen-nap, the lead ore containing silver would be extracted from the rocks by smelting.

Next, the lead would be smelted in a furnace at a higher temperature. The silver would separate from the lead and be poured into molds to form ingots.

Then the lead would be smelted again to remove impurities and poured into ingots. The Romans called the process cupellation.

When I informed William Saltash and John Chandler of the find, they informed me that the lead was almost as valuable as the silver.

We could sell all the lead ingots at ninety percent of the price of silver. That was an incredible price. I asked what they were used for and was told, 'drinking water piping.' I wish I hadn't asked.

I would sell the lead anyway.

My people were getting good at building furnaces. Six weeks later, we were pouring our first silver and lead ingots.

The lead was shipped to London using ships chartered by John Chandler. I was hoping that by using him as a cutout, it would be assumed that the lead was coming from several small pit mines.

Someone would want to take it if it were all associated with me. The authorities would impose a greater threat. Taxes. Taxmen would report all they saw to the Capitol.

I wasn't ready for that sort of scrutiny yet. My small army could defend against any of the locals, not the remnants of the Roman Empire.

My advisors and I discussed at length what to do with the silver. We could sell the ingots or stamp out coins.

We needed the coinage for our economy, but the right to stamp coins was jealously guarded. At first, only the Roman Emperor could mint coins.

As the Empire degraded, the right was given to the bishops. The bishops zealously enforced their rights more than the emperors.

Our Archbishop at Tintagel was worse than most. He would keep five percent of all silver sent for minting. Normally, it ran two to three percent.

The archbishop also practiced clipping the edges of the coin. It was more money in his pocket and devalued the coinage. As the only game in town, he could get away with it.

We, as a group, were not coming up with a solution. We would have to pay the archbishop's price.

Tom Smith grumbled, "We need our own Bishop."

I responded, "Brilliant, Tom. I wonder how much a Bishopric costs?"

Abbot Luke told us the Church was becoming more corrupt. The archbishop would sell a Bishopric for fifty thousand silvers.

"Based on our production estimates, it would be a five-year payback," I explained.

"I would also have to send one thousand silvers yearly to the archbishop each year," Abbott Luke told us.

I was glad to hear him verbally taking the position. Father Timothy was too young for the position. Not that young priests weren't promoted, but he didn't have the worldly experience needed.

Eleanor said, "Do you think we would be allowed to pay in installments of ten thousand silver a year?"

The economic discussions I had been having with my advisors were paying off.

When we had paid a Bishop to elevate Father Timothy, I hadn't paid attention to which Bishop it was.

In my parochial thinking, it was some Bishop in London or Lundenwic, as our locals called it.

Our Archbishop was in Tintagel, on the west coast of Cornwall. It was now the Capital of Dumnonii, having been moved from Exeter. I wanted nothing to do with Tintagel as it was about now that King Arthur of Legend was ruling.

I wondered if Merlin was another cast back in time.

It is a shame I had never read any books on premedieval England. When I asked, I was told Geraint was King and had lost a battle to King Ine of Wessex. No one seemed to know what that might mean for us. It was so far away. It was all of fifty miles.

John Chandler informed me that Armorica across the Channel was his major trading partner. London was becoming a crossroads for the Anglo-Saxons and had more trade with the remnants of the Roman Empire.

He thought Essex, who controlled London, would soon be absorbed by Mercia. Since Mercia and the Anglo-Saxons fought frequently, London would lose its newfound prominence.

London was almost deserted until the last hundred years. Now, it might fall again. That was hard to fathom as I remembered the London of my first life.

I asked Abbott Luke if it was possible to approach the archbishop about his being appointed Bishop of Cornwall.

"It would be better if it was Bishop of the Cornovii. The easterners look down upon members of our tribe. He wouldn't be as threatened by us backward people."

For some reason, I thought of Hillbillies.

"Please make inquiries. Don't speak of coinage. If he knew we had a good source of silver, he would never let us go."

"He will know of our selling books in London and assume I want a greater share of the newly found wealth in the area. I will draft a message and send it by boat to Tintagel."

I spoke up, "Tom can you make stamping dies to work with sheets of silver?"

"Yes, that will be no problem."

"How will you do it?

"We will roll a heated silver ingot into a sheet of the coin's thickness. Blanks will be cut out of the heated sheet. Like that thing you introduced to the cooks, a cookie cutter. The blanks will be placed in a die set and stamped out."

"Would it be possible to heat a metal sheet and pass it through a set of four dies that have pictures and wording on them? That way, you could stamp out four coins at once."

Tom frowned and thought for a few seconds.

"Four identical dies would be hard to achieve."

"The dies will have the engravings raised. Use a hardened steel die with a recessed engraving. Then, stamp unhardened steel to make multiple dies. Next, harden the multiple dies."

"That would work. Four dies at once would be best, so nothing would be off-center."

I then explained what a milled edge was. My advisors loved it. Our coins would be the best in the world.

I remembered that bad money chased good money out but kept silent.

An argument about what should be on either side of our coins broke out. I was against having my picture on them as they would be a trouble magnet, with me being the center of the trouble.

It made me realize I needed to be educated about the political situation in this time and place. I had made a lot of assumptions based on a minimum education in medieval England. I had thought the Romans left the area, and the Normans came shortly after that. Never realizing that London was not a true center of power.

I wondered what the rest of the world was like. I had all these plans and ideas without understanding what might come of introducing them. I needed to get my act together.

Eleanor was intrigued by the phrase. She didn't know I was an actor. It took me a while and many tickles in bed to explain it. I hoped for a son next time.

When it came time to decide what should be stamped on our coins, we had hours of discussion. My advisors had different opinions on what should be stamped on them. We kept the Monasteries illustrators busy creating samples of what we thought they should have.

One afternoon, I was picking up my latest version of the coins from the Monks and saw a new illustration.

It had Saint Piran's Flag on one side and a red-billed chough on the other. I asked about it, and the young monk (they are all young!) told me it was his idea.

We were growing the Barony of the Middle Counties by our mining, And Saint Piran is the patron saint of miners. The Palores, as he called it, was Cornish for digger, named after its digging for insects. He thought they symbolized what we were doing without offending the powers in Tintagel.

I presented his idea to the group, and they loved it. It was so well received because it got around our egos which became heavily involved.

We added the date and put his initials on the back. Heads were the bird, tails the flag. The one silver piece soon became known as crows. We couldn't color the bird's bill, so it looked like a crow.

Chapter 13

Our coins were eighty-five percent silver. This percentage seemed terrible to me, but melting out over a hundred different coins, we found they were eighty-three percent at best and some as low as seventy-five percent.

With the milled edges to show a coin had been clipped and our relatively high percentage of silver, our coins would be sought after. They would demand a premium over others.

We started with one silver denomination, then made half silver, quarter silver, one-tenth silver, five silver, and ten silver coins.

We also cast one penny coins out of bronze. All were the same as the original, just different sizes. Two half-silvers contained the same amount of silver as one silver. All were scaled in this manner like US coins used to be, or will be. Whatever.

The actual issuing of these coins would be some months in the future. It would take time to build the road and blast furnace needed, to roast the ore and cast enough coins to be worthwhile.

One of my projects had been to dictate a book on canning. This book was turned over to our chief health officer, Agnes. She had her people experiment with heat-processing food in glass jars reinforced with wire before sealing them with wax.

The processed jars were set aside for six months. When opened, the contents proved to be edible. The glasshouse had to increase production to meet the demand for the jars.

Beeswax was soon in short supply, so tallow from animal fats, mostly hogs, was used.

This method of storage would improve the food supply and health of the Barony. It would be some time before we could produce metal cans.

The first lead ore had been processed. Five tons of it had been roasted, yielding three tons of lead mixed with silver. When the silver was separated, we had 2,880 ounces of silver. This was two-point eight percent silver. My books reported results as high as five percent silver, so while great, it wasn't a record.

With the open pit mine being worked continuously and the ore being processed, we could generate eighty-six hundred ounces of silver monthly. My money worries were over, at least for a while.

Once we had blasting powder, production would go up dramatically. The mining of the ore was the bottleneck. We could always add another blast furnace and refining operation. Of course, opening another coal mine would probably be required, but we seemed to have coal in plenty.

Not all was work. We had time to play. I was focused on moving the Barony forward. Eleanor reminded me that we needed to reward the people for all their hard work.

Since it was the fall of 719, she suggested a harvest festival after the crops were in. This year would be the largest harvest in anyone's memory.

Not only would everyone be fed this winter, but an excess would be sent to London, Tintagel, and Armorica. This bountiful harvest would be remembered as a blessed year.

There was no reason that all years in the future wouldn't be like this, barring a drought.

The crops should all be in before the end of August. So, we could have a fair the next week. Our schools would resume the week following.

My advisors and I decided to hold the fair at Midpoint. That was the name that the pavilion at the border of Saltash and Owennap had been given, where our marriage had occurred.

Each District's wagon train would arrive the day before the fair. A team would stake out the camping sites for each District.

All merchants wanting a place at the fairgrounds were asked to let us know. There would be no charge, but we would plan a marketplace with orderly rows.

Agnes, or Lady Agnes as many were calling her, was in charge of laying out sanitation facilities and arranging for water towers to be set up and kept filled for the duration.

First aid stations would be set up along with a field hospital. We would use this as a prototype to accompany an army in the field.

I didn't explain why I named them MASH units. They were very helpful when they first formed in Korea. While not meeting a Hawkeye, I had an aide who put Radar to shame.

My contribution to the event planning was suggesting we have a parade one evening. The guilds from Saltash would be invited to have floats. I had to explain how floats were a traveling display of the guild's prowess.

There would be a beauty contest the night before, so there would be a float with the Queen of the Festival and her court. And then, I had to explain what a beauty contest was.

The army units would march at the front of the parade. Each District would have its own unit.

It was a shame, but there was no way we could have a marching band. Maybe next year.

When the word went out, there were many questions. Why hadn't we invited the Monastery to have a float? Weren't the Nurses good enough for their float?

We finally announced that any group who wanted to be in the parade was welcome. That was a mistake! The prostitutes from Saltash wanted in. Their float would be a huge bed pulled by two oxen.

There would be many contests, archery, crossbow marksmanship, dagger throwing, and foot races, both boys and girls. Even pie-eating contests.

For the younger children, piles of hay with coins were buried in them. Parents could drop their children off to play in the hay. The area would be roped off and controlled by the armsmen.

We would have armsmen walking the area. They even set up a temporary jail for the drunks to sleep it off.

I would cover all the costs.

The fair would be kicked off by Father Timothy giving a blessing the first evening, followed by a huge bonfire.

The fair was a huge success. All the planning paid off. There had been nothing like it in the memory of anyone living.

The archery contest was the most hard-fought. While not longbows, these guys could shoot far and accurately. I started telling Eleanor about Robin Hood but decided that might start something I would regret.

The crossbowmen and women were equally as good. We had a men's champion and a women's champion. We hadn't planned on it but had the men's and women's champions shoot off by popular demand.

The women won. You have never seen such cheering from all of the women present. The men sulked. It was so bad that I had to come up with another event.

It was a squad of men against a squad of women. The average of all their scores would determine the winners. I was glad to see the men win this one. The men felt vindicated, but the women had bragging rights.

A win-win. I noticed the two champions had gotten very close during the contest. I wondered how good their children might be.

By the time the children were grown, we might have rifles. Another story I didn't share was about William Tell and his son. I would lose half my troops if they heard that one.

The beauty contest was something to behold. The contest was a first. I had told Eleanor, who was in charge of the event, about the swimming suit judging, which was a no-go.

Then there was the talent contest. We had a laugh about who was the best milker or chicken girl then decided it wouldn't work either.

Then there was the question of judges. I flat-out refused to be involved. It was finally decided that they would be paraded in front of an audience. Whoever got the most cheers and applause would be the winner.

The judging taught me a lot about how women are viewed in this day and age. All the twenty entries were informed of the rules and were allowed to pick their own costumes.

Every one of them picked clothing that emphasized their busts and hips. Bras weren't around yet, so they wore a binding around their chests. Most of them forgot to bind themselves.

Judging by the crowd's noise, the event was a success. The winner was a young lady with the largest breast I had ever seen. Since she wasn't bound, she was a hazard as she walked, flopping everywhere.

Her hips were almost as large as her chest. She was built for having children and feeding them. I guess beauty is in the eye of the beholder. My Eleanor was only average looking by these standards. In my past life, she would have been considered a knockout.

The parade was a roaring success. My soldiers led the way, both men and women units. Some had to stay home to guard each of our Keeps, they lost in drawing straws.

The floats in the parade were ingenious. Thomas Smith had one of the better ones. He mounted a small forge complete with bellows and an anvil on a wagon and made horseshoes during the parade.

I'm glad I hadn't mentioned Mardi Gras and the throwing of plastic beads. He would have been throwing the hot horseshoes into the crowd.

Another float had two cows being milked. Father Timothy had an altar on his and probably prayed for all of us heathens. Abbott Luke, soon to be Bishop Luke, sat on a throne waving to the crowd.

All twenty beauty contestants with princess wreaths woven in their hair, were on a huge wagon drawn by six oxen. The Queen of the Parade wore a crown of beaten silver that Tom Smith had made. It was the winner's prize. It would feed her family for a year in need.

Eleanor informed me that all the contestants had received marriage proposals. Good ones! They were much better than if they had only stayed in their small areas. I suspect we will have hundreds of contestants next year.

Eleanor and I decided to make this an annual event. Sitting on our viewing stand, watching the people pass by, we realized it was bringing our people together.

Even the pickpockets from Saltash were working together. We knew this because so many had been arrested. They would be sentenced to work on one of the road crews, if they ran off. It would be no loss to us.

The only sour note was that three little girls no older than three were found abandoned.

The three-year-old knew her first name; her mother was Mama, and she had no Daddy. They became the first occupants of the orphanage we would build in Owen-nap. In the meantime, Agnes and her nurses would see to the little ones.

As anticipated, the drunk tank was full night after night. Only a few of the drunks were surly. Most slept it off and were released in the morning. The grumpy ones were kept an extra day. We kept a record of them, and they were told if they returned, it was the road crews for them.

Only one caused more problems, he fought our event police. The offender received a blow to the head in the fight and died the next day. No great loss.

Waste wagons were brought in and filled to the brim on the last day. All the event debris was stacked in the middle of a field, and we held a huge bonfire.

I had a surprise up my sleeve. It was nothing by my standards of a fireworks show, but it was amazing in this day and age. Enough gunpowder had been made for three crude rockets to be launched. They were glorified bottle rockets, only going up a hundred feet or so before exploding. But they gave a huge flash and a bang.

You would have thought the world was coming to an end. People were running and screaming. Animals were jumping, mooing, and neighing. Sheep were baaing, pigs oinking. It was magnificent.

That was until Eleanor gave me an earful.

Chapter 14

All was going so well that I was waiting for the other shoe to drop. It only took a week. Settled back in at Owen-nap, a rider came thundering into the courtyard, yelling that we had been attacked.

Eleanor, John, and I ran out to the courtyard to see what all the noise was about. The rider gasped for breath, so he was brought an ale to help his throat.

He gasped. "A group of soldiers was spotted coming from the west. Our scouts managed to warn the miners in time to put your plan into effect."

"Did the scouts tell you how many soldiers there were?"

"Between fifty and sixty, My Lord."

That would have been too many for the miners and guards to stand off. They did the right thing. Since we hadn't finished our Keep there yet, my advisors and I had devised a plan in case this happened.

The scouts were watching the passes two days out from the mine. If anyone was spotted coming through, they were to give the camp a warning. Depending on how many and their composition, the miners had options ranging from preparing a welcome dinner to abandoning the camp.

They did the right thing by retreating to Bodmin. They packed up their tools, destroyed all foodstuffs they didn't have room for, and left. By the time the enemy troops had arrived, they were safely back in Bodmin.

I urgently met with Eleanor, John, Thomas, Father Timothy, and Abbot Luke. There wasn't time to bring in John Chandler or my father-in-law. We decided that the emergency plan we had previously discussed would be appropriate.

Riders were sent to all Districts Keeps informing them of the invasion. They were to send ten armsmen to Bodmin to check their Keeps' food and water supplies. All their people were to be notified, and scouts were to watch all border crossings.

At Owen-nap, we assembled a supply train to accompany our troops to Bodmin. We would field an army of one hundred men with the outlying District's troops. Forty spearmen and sixty archers. There would also be cooks and other support people with the supply train, adding another fifty people to our group.

The train itself would carry thirty days of food for everyone. Wagons and beasts to pull them were already stationed at Owen-nap. All those courses on logistics at West Point were paying off.

From the scout's reports, the enemy was coming from the direction of Hilston. That didn't mean they were from Hilston, but we had to find out quickly. Two riders each were sent to Brude and Looe.

One rider approached the village, and the other remained distant to observe the first rider's reception. Once it was known how the first rider was received, they or the second rider would return to Bodmin.

Five days had passed since the scout had arrived with the news of the invasion and our arrival at Bodmin. Eleanor stayed at our Keep with the baby.

The troops from the districts had all arrived. I went over my plan with the Sergeants. It was not going to be a head-on attack. We would surround the troops who had seized the pit mine. There would be no attack, I only wanted to pin them in place.

As ordered, the miners had set all the buildings on fire as they left. No shelter, food, or tools were left for the invaders.

The invading army of forty men had set up a tent encampment at the entrance to the pit. It was only four feet deep, covering an area about the size of a football field. There was a road cut to allow wagons to go down into the pit. The road would circle the sides as the cut went down.

Depending on the ore field, the mine might have to be widened, and the roads moved to the new sides.

Human nature being what it is, the foreign army had set their tents up at the entrance to the pit. No tents were in the pit because of water draining into it.

We would have a water problem when the pit was about twenty feet deep. The pit was on a slope, so we planned a cut at the lower end to drain the water. Since there was no cut yet, any rain would accumulate in the pit.

That gave me a thought.

"Sergeant Stoneman, please station your troops west of the pit. That puts the tents between you and the pit opening. The plan is to drive the enemy into the pit and separate them from what food and shelter they have."

"Aye, My Lord," softly replied the Sergeant.

We had all our troops move into position. Once the Sergeant indicated they were ready, I yelled, "Fire".

Sixty crossbows gave off their distinctive twang. The enemy had most of their soldiers in the pit using small hand tools to chip out ore.

The four on top died at once. My spearmen advanced as the crossbowmen reloaded. Several of the enemy came running out of their tents and made it to the pit before they could be fired upon.

When our spearmen reached the tents, they pulled them down. There were loose rocks from the pit lying around. They started to build a wall facing the pit opening. The enemy couldn't escape the pit without being under our fire.

We had them trapped.

The scouts who had observed them reported no supply train accompanying them. What food they had was in their packs. That meant a supply train would be following.

I planned to intercept that supply train. We would then starve out the troops at the pit mine. Harsh, but fewer lives were lost on our side.

Leaving forty armsmen to pin the invaders in place. I led the other sixty to a pass the relieving supply train must go through.

We had to get to that pass first. If the supply train was from Hilston, I estimated they would reach the pass at about the same time as us. We would have to march late into the day and set up an ambush upon arrival.

I had guessed wrong. My scouts reported the supply train was exiting the pass while we were still hours away.

That was the bad news. The good news was that only twenty additional troops accompanied them. They were being sloppy. They didn't have scouts of their own out.

After a quick conference with the Sergeants, I ordered an L-shaped ambush. Because of the terrain, it wouldn't be much of a surprise.

Ten of us formed the lower bar of the L by standing across the road. The rest of the troops hid by the side of it. Their guards charged us when they saw us standing across the road, blocking it.

That was their last charge because the ambush was sprung as soon as they were clear of the long line of wagons.

The crossbowmen took the charging guards down in one volley. The wagon drivers surrendered as they were grossly outnumbered.

Altogether, there were twenty-seven wagons full of food and mining equipment. We cleaned up the battlefield, digging a shallow grave for the guards. It had to be shallow as this part of the mountain was mostly stone.

We left the wagon drivers in place with our people riding with them. It took us a full day to get back to the pit mine. Scouts were left at the pass to bring word of any follow-up troops.

Our people on the wagons were told to converse with their drivers. We needed to know where they came from and as much information about their home Keep or Keeps as possible.

I had watched enough detective stories on TV to know that you interviewed people separately and compared stories. This method would give the best picture. I would have loved to pull a Columbo, but it wasn't in the cards.

When we returned to the pit mine, all was the same as when we left. The invaders still held the mine but couldn't leave. They had to be getting hungry.

The multiple separate interviews revealed that this was Hilston's only operation. Their Baron had sent most of his troops on the first strike and followed up with the rest with his supply train.

According to the people we interrogated, less than ten armsmen remained at the Hilston Keep.

I couldn't fathom why the Baron would have done it this way. It was a roll of the dice that would destroy his Barony if he lost. They had lost, but it still made no sense.

I asked for the highest-ranking prisoner to be brought to me. There was one Sergeant.

"Sergeant, I fail to understand why this attack was made. It was bound to fail and end up in disaster for your Baron. Can you explain?"

The Sergeant stared at the ground, then looked up and said, "It doesn't matter now. I will tell you the story."

He continued. "Our crops have failed. We don't have enough food to get us through the winter. Most people would die. Our young Baron wanted to ask you and others for help. Brude turned us down. Liskeard has the same problem.

"Baron Hilston wanted to ask you for help, but his Steward, his Uncle, wouldn't let the young man send messengers."

"Our scouts knew of your lead find, so the Uncle decided we would raid the mine, taking enough lead ore to sell in Tintagel for food. There was no intention of trying to hold the mine."

"How old is the Baron?"

"Fourteen, My Lord."

"Where is his Uncle?"

"I presume in the pit with the others."

"I would like to show you some things."

My soldiers had looted the effects of the ones we had killed in the original volley. All except one, who was armed and dressed better than the others. His arms had been brought to me.

The Sergeant recognized them as belonging to the Uncle.

"Sergeant, I have no desire to kill the people in the pit. Will you talk to them and tell them to surrender, or we will starve them out."

"What will happen to them?"

"They will accompany us to Hilston, where I need to talk to your Baron."

"I will do that, My Lord."

I picked up that he was calling me, My Lord. I think he saw the writing on the wall. Not that he was correct, but at least he was thinking.

We gave him a white flag to carry. It was a small piece of sheep fleece nailed to a spear.

He wasn't in the pit very long when the soldiers followed him out, leaving their weapons behind.

My people collected the weapons while I ordered our cooks to feed the prisoners. Thankfully, none of my people had been killed. Property destroyed, yes.

Eleanor and I had many a bedroom discussion on what sort of ruler I needed to be. My inclinations were much milder than these harsh times. She finally agreed my way may be better.

If nothing else, my way wouldn't set up long-lasting feuds. At best, we would have long-term allies. How we treated people would affect the thinking of the next group we met. I may be naïve to think that. Eleanor thought that they would see me as soft. We will see.

I returned a message to Bodmin informing Eleanor and my staff of the situation. I was leaving the pit defended by a light force and continuing to Hilston.

The trip was interesting. We went through a narrow, deep pass with a quartz vein about seven feet tall and fifty yards wide.

It met the textbook conditions for gold. I would have to have samples taken. But first, I must settle the Hilston matter.

The village at Hilston was silent, with no one in sight. The villagers were either hiding in their homes or had fled.

Chapter 15

Coming to the entrance of the Keep, we found a young man standing in the doorway unaccompanied. He didn't look like anything special. He was average size for the area with average looks.

He had a resigned look on his face. He probably thought he was going to die in the next few minutes.

Going up to him, I said, "Baron Hilston, I presume?"

"Yes, all I ask is that you spare my people."

"I understand that you wanted to ask us for help as your crops failed, but your uncle decided to try to take enough lead to sell and feed the people."

"If you take Hilston, will you prevent my people from starving?"

"Your people will be fed."

"Then it works out for the best."

"The only problem is that I won't kill you."

"What is to be my fate?"

"Let's go inside the Keep and discuss your future."

After we were settled inside the Keep's office, we continued our discussion.

"What do you want?" I asked.

"I know I don't want to be the Baron. It is too much of a burden. My parents died last year of the grippe, and I had to take their place. My Uncle has been doing the work, and I suspect he wants to be Baron Hilston. I may not have long to live."

"Your Uncle is dead. Your people won't starve. The only question is if you should remain in power or become part of my lands."

"I don't want to remain in power. I don't know what to do."

"That makes you wiser than most."

Their situation turned out to be simple. They were flat broke and didn't have enough food to feed their people halfway through the winter.

The deceased Uncle had a wife and two sons. I asked to meet with them. They could be a problem.

The boy's aunt and two male cousins were belligerent. They told me everything that went wrong was the boy's fault. All would have been well if he had given his uncle his way.

I didn't understand that logic as the uncle did things his way, and they saw how that turned out. His aunt asked if they could leave Hilston and go to Tintagel, where her parents lived. I gave them my blessing and urged them to leave soon. I probably should have had them strangled and buried.

Baron Hilston showed me the village granary. It was in worse condition than what he had told me. The village Headman joined us and told me about how the farms were all in terrible condition. The previous Baron had done nothing to try to improve their lot in life. Again, that made no sense as they were in a downward spiral.

Rescuing Baronies was getting to be routine. Thad had orders for food supplies written out when we returned to the Keep. He also had a list of trades that needed help.

Later that evening, the Baron, the village Headman, and I continued our conversations about local conditions.

The Headman asked, "Are you going to help Liskeard?"

"I wasn't aware they needed help."

"They also had a crop failure this year. The cities on this side of the mountains didn't get rain."

"We need to talk to them before they do something rash. Baron Hilston, would you please send one of your men to Baron Liskeard to inform him that I'm willing to provide grain? Would he please send a delegation to discuss the matter?"

"Yes, My Lord."

"That answer leads us to our next conversation. Please have your Senior Sergeant join us."

At least he didn't use the same words as he summoned the Sergeant over to us. I told Thad to take a complete record of this. Once we were gathered, I told them the purpose of this meeting.

"There is the question of what to do with Hilston and Baron Hilston going forward. I see several options. It can remain a separate independent Barony without treaties with us, become an Ally, or be incorporated into my domain."

The Sergeant exclaimed, "You would give us these options?"

"Yes, it will cost me less if you are a willing partner in this rather than creating future problems."

"What about me?" asked the young Baron.

"You remain, Baron if you choose complete independence, the same if you are Allied with us. If you choose to become part of us, you will lose the title of Baron but will remain here learning to run the new District."

"How would I learn to run this new District?"

"You would become an aide to one of my Senior Sergeants who would be in charge."

I turned to the Baron's Senior Sergeant.

"I don't intend to insult you, Sergeant, but I suspect you have never had the authority or training to run the Barony. However, you will be in charge of the rebuilt defense forces."

The Sergeant nodded his understanding.

"You are correct, My Lord."

The Headman asked, "What of the villagers and farmers?"

"You, your wife, the senior midwife, and the best farmers will travel to Owen-nap to see what we have done. The Sergeant and Baron will accompany you. Once you understand the benefits, we will help you adopt our ways.

"You don't have to tell me which way you want to proceed until after your trip."

It took several days for them to get ready for their trip. An escort would be provided to ensure their safety. If they died along the way, I would be blamed and villainized.

The day before they left, Baron Liskeard showed up with a small entourage. I had expected a representative, but this made things simpler.

After welcoming them and getting them settled into the Keep and fed, I left them alone with the Baron and the group going to Owen-nap so that Baron Hilston could explain in private what was happening.

I noticed when we fed the group, they ate like they had missed a few meals. Not starving, but on the verge.

The next morning, Baron Liskeard asked for a private meeting. When alone, I waited for him to begin. As a General in the US Army, I learned that he who spoke first usually lost in negotiations. It seemed the Baron had learned the same lesson as we stared at each other.

I finally snorted and said, "What do you have in mind? We could play this game all day."

The Baron was a capable-looking man in his early forties, not an inexperienced youth.

He did look a little youthful as he grinned and replied, "I had to try to gain some position as you clearly have the upper hand."

"Things are that bad?"

"Worse, we have almost eaten the entire crop we managed to bring in. My Barony will be starving in weeks. I need your help."

"Help comes at a price."

"I will pay the price. I love my people more than my pride."

"Your people won't starve no matter what is decided here. I see two options. You can remain independent and pay over time for our help. Two, you become part of my

Barony and owe nothing. Unlike Baron Hilston, you can run your Barony."

"There is a third option, My Lord."

"What is that?"

"We remain independent, and I owe you allegiance as My Lord. That way, you will have to provide us with food without repayment. As a vassal, I will owe you troops, to support your endeavors."

His proposal took me aback. Eleanor and I had discussed the possibility of having vassals. The pro was that it would make me stronger without having battles. The con was that it would bring me to the attention of Tintagel.

The way things were proceeding, Tintagel would be fully aware of the expansion of my Barony and would be taking steps to curb my power. There would be nothing lost by taking Liskeard as a vassal.

I would have to assume a title, a Baron being a vassal to a Baron, would be too confusing. At least confusing to this time and place. The title I would adopt would not have been used before. I always got the actual titles mixed up in my internal translation.

Locally they only had two levels of titles between Baron and Emperor. Even the title Emperor was a bit dodgy as no one wanted that target on their back, so there were several variations.

I could go with Baron, Viscount, Count, Earl, Duke, King, and Emperor. Those had worked in the medieval ages, so I adopted them for now.

"Baron Liskeard, I accept you being a vassal on your terms. I'm to be addressed as Viscount Owen-Nap. We will have a formal ceremony at Liskeard in front of your people. In the meantime, let's get together orders for a grain caravan."

I would also have Baron Hilston make vows to me. Eleanor would be pleased with these events. She had been pushing me to take more power in the area.

Chapter 16

In the Barony of Looe, another conversation was occurring.

"Baron Looe, we have heard from Padstow and Bolventor. They both refuse to participate in any effort to conquer Baron Owen-nap."

"Fools! There is great wealth there for the taking. However, we don't have enough troops to overcome those new crossbowmen."

"We could do it another way, My Lord," stated his steward.

"What is that?"

"The word is that he is besotted with his new wife. With her in hand, we could dictate terms."

"Are you certain?"

"My spies are convinced that he will bend to our will."

"I'm to know nothing of this. If it fails, it is all on your head."

"Yes, My Lord."

"You may go now, do what you must do."

On my way out, I thought, 'I will do what I must do, you old fool. Once we have the wife, I won't need you. Your head Sergeant is mine. I shall have all.'

*****

Eleanor

In Bodmin, a third conversation occurred.

Sara Farmer, head of the Baroness Own, was explaining.

"Ladies, we can never tell when we might be betrayed. You must have a secret weapon and know how to use it against need."

Me, my friend Anne, maid Marion, Johanna Farmer, the baby's nurse, and Janet Farmer, baby Catherine's bodyguard, were present.

While Janet Farmer bristled with weapons, the rest of us shrank back from the wicked-looking six-inch long dagger Sara held.

"You will not be expected to use this in a knife fight. There is no time to get you ready for that. We can teach you where to stick it in a man's body to do the most good."

She showed them the kidneys and how to cut a man's throat.

"There are other fatal spots, such as the major arteries in the leg, but they take too long. The man may kill you or yell for help. Cutting his throat is preferred as it is quick and prevents them from yelling. Of course, you need to do this by surprise. Face to face, you won't have a chance, well, unless you can stick it in his eye, but then he will make a lot of noise. Better by stealth."

She then handed out a similar dagger to each of the ladies. All took them though the nurse looked like she was picking up a poison snake.

Janet Farmer sneered at the short daggers as she displayed hers. It was almost a small sword.

Sara told Janet, "If they need to use theirs, it is because you are not there or are already dead."

Janet mumbled as she sheathed her dagger, "Yes, Ma'am."

Sara then handed each woman a sheath with a small belt around each lady's leg.

"You will wear these at all times. It is a case of when you need it. You will need it right then. No going to your room for a change."

"Lady Eleanor here is a second knife for you."

The knife's blade was only two inches long.

"We call it a hideout knife. If you are searched, and your searcher finds the one on your leg, he will think you to be disarmed. This knife will also cut a throat."

"Where will I hide it?"

"Between and low on your breast."

"That will surprise James!"

The ladies all giggled at that thought.

Sara continued, "You will wear these pins in your hair."

The pins were steel and long enough to pierce a man's eye and reach the brain. Their use is obvious.

The last item she handed me was a curious rope to use as a second belt.

"We call this a garotte. I will show you how to use it."

"I hope we never have to use any of these.

"So do I, My Lady."

***** Steward at Looe

I shared my plan with my Sergeant.

"The old Baron at Bodmin had a secret passage dug as an escape route. When he died, the secret died with all but the old Sergeant in charge of the dig. The Sergeant came to me and offered to show me the exit, which would be our entrance. He wanted a thousand silver for the information. I told him I would pay for it. He showed me, and I gave him one thousand silvers."

"You actually paid him?"

"Of course, I'm a man of my word. Since I had made no promises of what would

151

happen after he was paid, I killed him, and took the silver back."

A nervous-looking Sergeant replied, "Well done, My Lord."

"We will use the hidden entrance, which takes us directly to the Baron's chambers. I have checked, and that is where Lady Owen-nap will be staying."

"When do we go, My Lord."

"She arrives tomorrow. You keep calling me My Lord. I'm not your Lord yet."

"Yes, My Lord."

I gave a small chuckle. I was glad to see the Sergeant understood the situation.

"When we capture Lady Owen-nap, what do we do with any others in her chambers?"

"We don't need them. Kill them."

"Even her baby?"

"Especially the baby. We don't want any followers to use her as a symbol."

"Yes, My Lord."

"Now go and prepare your men."

"There will be five of us, My Lord. If we needed more, the mission would be a failure."

'See that you don't fail!"

At that, the Sergeant left.

Talking to myself , I said, "Now when to kill Baron Looe and take power."

*****

Lady Eleanor

Johanna Farmer asked where baby-wet Catherine was to sleep.

"In here with me, of course."

"There is a small room to the side that we could use. That way, if she awakes in the night, I can feed her without waking all."

"That would be good. Make it so."

Janet Farmer, Catherine's bodyguard, checked out the room.

"It is a good defensive point. The door can be barred from the inside and is stout enough that it would take a battering ram to break through. Also, there is a heavy wardrobe that can have round wooden pieces placed under it so that it can be quickly rolled into place, further blocking the door."

"Well thought Janet," I said.

I will sleep on this side of the door to guard it and help protect you."

"Is that necessary? My Lord James, insists that two guards are always outside my door and another two inside at night?"

"We don't know who may be planning evil, and Bodmin is strange territory to us, so we must take precautions."

"I guess, though it seems excessive. It would take an army to get through the Keep, much less this room."

*****

Looe's Sergeant

My five soldiers and I were shown the entrance to the escape tunnel by the Steward that night. The entrance or exit, as you will, was inside an abandoned cottage. It looked like the house for a failed farm.

The Steward didn't wish us luck or any other words of encouragement as we entered the narrow tunnel. The men carried two torches as they squished through the mud of the poorly drained works. After half an hour and a quarter mile, we reached the end of the tunnel.

Placing the torches in wall holders, we climbed the stairs to the second floor of the Keep. There was a small landing at the top of the stairs.

When the last man arrived, I lifted a latch on a wooden panel. It was the back of a cupboard used for storing clothes.

Making certain my men had their weapons ready, I burst out of the cupboard. The scene before me was dimly lit by a small lantern.

There were two guards standing, facing the door where they thought any enemies might come through.

The third guard was asleep in a chair. They had been taking turns throughout the night. Facing the wrong way costs them. They were cut down as they tried to draw their weapons while turning.

*****As put together later.

Unseen Janet Farmer was standing in the doorway to the side room where baby Catherine slept. Janet knew her duty though it broke her heart. She stood back and closed, then barred the door into the baby's room. Next, she moved the large cupboard on its rollers in front of the door.

Lady Eleanor was waking up to the noise of the battle around her. By the time she was awake, she was roughly seized and wrapped in a blanket.

The room's security now worked against her as the guards outside of her room tried to break the barred bedroom door. They wouldn't be through in time.

When they finally entered the room, they found the bodies of three dead guards and no sign of Lady Eleanor.

A quick search found the cupboard they had entered through. Sending for torches to light their way, the guards entered the tunnel only to find that it had been collapsed behind the escaping interlopers.

155

Search parties were sent out but found no trail in the darkness.

An exultant Steward was waiting for us when we reached the tunnel exit. We had our prize with no losses, not that he cared about any losses. That there were no bodies left behind to identify the attackers was what mattered.

The Steward was not happy to learn that Catherine hadn't been killed, but that was a minor matter which could be rectified later.

The blanket that Lady Eleanor was wrapped in yielded a furious lady. She had a short dagger in hand and managed to knife one of her captors in the stomach. He would die in pain later.

The other guards disarmed her and brought her to her knees.

The Steward spoke up, "Now that wasn't very ladylike, My Lady."

Eleanor's response was not fit for polite company.

"Tsk, tsk, what language? Bind her mouth, Sergeant, then search her for more weapons."

After tying a cloth tightly around Eleanor's mouth, I roughly searched her, finding a two-inch blade hanging low between her breasts.

It was a two-day journey to Looe, and Lady Eleanor was kept bound and watched carefully even when relieving herself. The man she had stabbed died on the second day. Making her treatment even rougher.

The Steward let us do all but rape her. He wanted her in good condition when her husband surrendered to him. After that, he might pleasure himself with her.

Chapter 17

I was in a meeting on the second day when two messengers arrived. They had ridden their horses to a lather. One of the horses would probably die.

The messengers were brought to me immediately with the dire news that his Lady had been seized and taken away.

Baby Catherine was left behind in good health due to the quick thinking of her guard, Janet Farmer.

Troops searched for any sign of Eleanor's captors, but Sara Farmer's people found no traces.

Only fifty-some years of soldiering kept me calm. I knew what could be done was being done.

I and fifty of his troops were bound for Bodmin within the hour. Not double-timing their march but keeping it up hour after hour-long into the night. We marched by the light of the moon, dealing death on every mind.

We made the mine pit late in the night. Resting for a few hours, then moving again at dawn's first hint of light. We arrived at

Bodmin at the end of the third day. It would normally be considered a five-day trip.

Sara Farmer was waiting for me.

"The raiders knew of a secret entrance to Bodmin Keep. They blocked the way in their escape. It has taken us several days, but we have found the exit to the secret tunnel, along with evidence of violence."

"Take me there."

"Do you need to rest?"

"Not yet. Let me see what was left. Then I must rest."

"Very well, follow me."

Horses had been brought out for them. It was just as well as I probably couldn't have walked much further.

The small, abandoned cottage that concealed the tunnel exit was a short ride but a long walk away. Once there, we dismounted.

A squad of ten guards was protecting the area. There was blood on the floor inside the cottage.

Sara Farmer directed my attention to a dagger lying on the floor.

"That is Eleanors," I exclaimed.

"She must have wounded one of them."

She then pointed to a blanket.

"It appears My Lady was brought here in that and attacked one of them when freed.

There is a trail of blood leaving here. Scouts are following it. They have a five-day head start, so we cannot catch them. But we will know where they went."

I nodded. "We will return to the Keep. I do need the rest. Wake me as soon as we know where they are bound."

I slept restlessly through the afternoon and the following night. Upon waking, I felt terrible, like I had been awake the whole time.

I called Sara Farmer and asked for an update.

"One of the scouts has returned with information. Lady Eleanor is alive with her captors. She wounded one they took with them. He died on the way, and they left his body in a ditch."

"The other scout is still tracking them and leaving his trail well-marked so we may follow. They were heading towards Looe's."

"Then let us be on our way."

"You must eat first, My Lord."

This formality by Sara Farmer reminded me that I needed to listen to her. I was too worked up to think clearly.

"Very well, let's eat, but be quick about it."

I ate like a ravening wolf.

As he ate, other actions were taking place in Looe.

I brought Lady Eleanor to Baron Looe's.

"Here is the Lady you asked for, My Lord."

"Good, you are dismissed. I will take it from here."

Instead of leaving, I approached the Baron.

"What is this, Steward? You forget your place."

"You have a new place, My Lord."

I pulled a dagger and stabbed the Baron to death.

"Your new place is Hell, you old fool."

I turned to my accompanying guards.

"Lock her in a cell, then remove this piece of trash."

"Yes, My Lord Looe."

At that, I, the new Baron, smiled. My plan was working, now to bring Baron Owen-nap to heel.

*****

Lady Eleanor

I was taken to a cell in the Keep, as there was no dungeon. I could see the soldier's barracks out of my barred window. After watching for several hours, I determined that there were about forty armsmen in residence. The servants carried things from my right and returned empty-handed to the left.

There was one jailor outside of the cell. The cell itself was a small six-foot by six-foot room. Most men wouldn't have been able to sleep on the filthy pallet.

My older guard, jailor, was fat and ugly, to say the least. He stank so bad I could smell him six feet away. His teeth were rotten, and his clothes held the remnants of many meals.

He kept rattling the keys on his belt as he talked, as though he would let me out if I yielded to him.

He kept making lurid suggestions. When I had seen as much of the Keep's manpower as I could, I approached the bars.

"I have something for you."

He crossed a few feet to me quickly.

"What?"

"This."

I rammed one of my steel hairpins into his eye and grabbed his tunic to keep him from falling away from the cell door.

Unlocking the crude lock on the cell, I made my escape. The outer door to my cell room was standing wide open. I had little time.

Anyone passing by would see I was out. There was no place to hide my jailor's body, and I had no time.

Heading left, I was shortly led to a kitchen and workshop where servants clustered together and talking. The real Baron had just been murdered and replaced by the hated Head Steward.

One of the serving girls gasped as she spotted me. The others turned to see what was going on.

I told them, "I need your help."

The servants stood there, not knowing what to do. A rotund woman took charge.

"Girls, she needs to be cleaned and fresh clothes."

As the maids took me in hand, the cook continued.

"Giles, check on the jail. If there is a body, as I expect, hide it."

Turning to me, she said, "The old Baron was a bastard, but he was our bastard. All we ask Lady Eleanor is for you to bring your forces and kill the Steward."

I asked, "How do you know who I am?"

"We have seen copies of the Owen-nap newspaper with your picture in it."

The cook told me, "We will help you if you help us."

"What help do you need?"

"Get rid of the Head Steward. Our former Baron wasn't good, but this man is evil."

"Do the troops support the Head Steward?"

"No, only his Sergeant and four others; there were five, but I understand that you killed one of them."

"When they entered my chamber by a secret passage, I fought and knifed one of them. He died of his wounds."

"Good, he was the worst of the soldiers."

"Will any of the soldiers help me?"

"Yes, but they need a plan."

I thought for a minute.

"Where is the Steward now?"

"He will be in the old Baron's office. He gives orders from there."

"What guards does he have?"

"There will be two outside the entrance door and two in the room with him."

"Will they be those that are loyal to him?"

"The ones inside, the outside are ordinary armsmen."

"Where will the other two guards be?"

"Probably drinking ale in the main hall."

"Could you please have someone confirm that?"

"At once, My Lady."

They gave me a slice of ham, some cheese, and freshly baked bread while we waited. A few minutes later, a scullery maid returned, confirming that the two guards were drunk in the main hall.

Thinking for a minute, I came up with a plan.

"Here is what we will do."

The plan was simple: four guards would capture the drunks in the hall. They would be placed in the jail cell. If they had any problems, they were to be killed.

I was given a dagger, and my wrists bound tightly. It would look like I was restrained but could drop the cords easily.

The men in the main hall were killed trying to escape capture.

The four guards took me to the old Baron's office. One on each side of me and two behind.

At the door to the office, one of the guards, a Sergeant, whispered to the door guards. They nodded their heads and knocked on the office door.

When told to enter, they pushed me through the opening, just enough to move me into the room.

The Head Steward who had stood to see what was happening.

The Sergeant spoke, "We found her in the hall. She killed her jailor and escaped.

"Well done, Sergeant. You will be rewarded."

"This is all the reward I need."

The Sergeant and the guard behind him attacked the Steward's guard on his left side. The guards on my side attacked the other guard.

I dropped the cords from my wrists and brought the dagger I held in my long sleeves up into the Steward's throat.

Being taught to strike as hard as I could, I struck him under his jaw, driving the blade into his brain. He fell dead at my feet.

The last two guards died easily at the hands of their four attackers.

Once they were dead, I asked,

"Now what?"

The old Sergeant who had helped her said, "The Barony is now yours by right of conquest."

"How can that be, I'm a lone woman, and you have many armsmen."

"But we have no one who can lead us. The old Baron had no living children and had trained no one to succeed him. We would fall into anarchy if someone didn't take charge. We have seen what Owen-nap has accomplished and wish to be part of that.

"The old Baron was stubborn in his ways but saw things had to change; he just didn't know how. The Head Steward, as you know, plotted to take power by capturing you. He couldn't have made a worse mistake."

I asked, "Will others go along with this?"

The Sergeant answered. "With great fervor, My Lady. We all know the great strides that Baron Owen-nap has made and how he takes care of his people. Those who can read have been sharing your newspapers with all our people. We have had to do it secretly, but no one has turned us in for doing so. We want to join your successful Barony."

I led my soldiers to the village of Looe. The streets were deserted, so there was no one to stop us.

We proceeded to the main gate of the Keep, where a lone figure stood at the entrance. The advance scouts gasped and ran back to me.

"My Lord, Lady Eleanor stands by herself in the entrance to the Keep."

"Does it appear to be a trap?"

As this information was being transmitted, Lady Eleanor walked up to us.

"Husband, I give you the Barony of Looe by right of conquest."

I dismounted and brought her into my arms.

"I was so scared for you. Right of conquest? There has to be a tale there."

"There is. Let's go to my office, and I will share it."

We walked arm and arm into the old Baron's office. Once the door was closed, Eleanor broke down into tears.

"I was so scared. I didn't know what to do."

"You seemed to have figured it out."

"It was mostly reacting. First, we were attacked, and I stabbed that horrid man. Then, I was in a jail cell and had to get out. I used the hairpins that Sara gave me. The cook and Sergeant offered to help. It all happened so fast I didn't have time to think."

"Dear, that is what battle is like. If you don't react, you die. You did well."

"I don't want to go through this again."

"I don't want you to go through it again, but we must always be prepared for something like this."

We stood there in a tight hug for what seemed forever but was only a few minutes. We parted, and she gave me more information about the Barony.

Chapter 18

A knock on the door brought us back to the world.

John Steward walked in.

"My Lord, Thad and I have sent the normal orders to start bringing this Barony under your control. The people are in better shape than Hilston and Liskeard, so that isn't as much of an issue."

"Well done, John, now we need a man to take command here. Eleanor has told me the Sergeant who helped her is old and should be retired with honor."

"Sergeant Treleaven at Bodmin is the best choice for the job. He has a level head on his shoulders and can make things happen."

"Very well, have him and his family moved here if willing. The usual payments."

And just like that, another Barony had been added to my lands. If this kept up, I would have to be called Count rather than Viscount.

Lady Eleanor

Lady Eleanor had just been asked by her nurse, Johanna Farmer, where baby-wet Catherine was to sleep.

"In here with me, of course."

"There is a small room to the side that we could use. That way, if she awakes in the night, I can feed her without waking all."

"That would be good. Make it so."

Janet Farmer, Catherine's bodyguard, checked out the room.

"It is a good defensive point. The door can be barred from the inside and is stout enough that it would take a battering ram to break through. Also, there is a heavy wardrobe that can have round wooden pieces placed under it so that it can be quickly rolled into place, further blocking the door."

"Well thought Janet," said Lady Eleanor.

I will sleep on this side of the door to guard it and help protect you."

"Is that necessary, My Lord James, insists that two guards are outside my door at all times and another two inside at night?"

"We don't know who may be planning evil, and this is strange territory to us, so we must take precautions."

"I guess, though it seems excessive. It would take an army to get through the Keep, much less this room."

The Looe's Sergeant and his five soldiers were shown the entrance to the escape tunnel by the Steward that night. The entrance or exit, as you will, was inside an abandoned cottage. It looked like the house for a failed farm.

The Steward didn't wish them luck or any other words of encouragement as they entered the narrow tunnel. The men carried two torches as they squished through the mud of the poorly drained works. After half an hour and a quarter mile, they reached the end of the tunnel.

Placing the torches in wall holders, they climbed the stairs to the second floor of the Keep. There was a small landing at the top of the stairs.

When the last man arrived, the Sergeant lifted a latch on a wooden panel. It was the back of a cupboard used for storing clothes.

Making certain his men had their weapons ready, he burst out of the cupboard. The scene before him was dimly lit by a small lantern. There were two guards standing, facing the door where they thought any enemies might come through.

The third guard was asleep in a chair. They had been taking turns throughout the night. Facing the wrong way costs them. They were cut down as they tried to draw their weapons while turning.

Unseen Janet Farmer was standing in the doorway to the side room where baby Catherine slept. Janet knew her duty, though it broke her heart. She stood back and closed, then barred the door into the baby's room. Next, she moved the large cupboard on its rollers in front of the door.

Back in the first room, Lady Eleanor was waking up to the noise of the battle around her. By the time she was awake, she was roughly seized and wrapped in a blanket.

The room's security now worked against her as the guards outside of her room tried to break the barred bedroom door. They wouldn't be in time.

When they finally entered the room, they found the bodies of three dead guards. Of Lady Eleanor, there was no sign.

A quick search found the cupboard they had entered through. Sending for torches to light their way, the guards entered the tunnel only to find that it had been collapsed behind the escaping interlopers.

Search parties were sent out but didn't find any trail in the darkness.

By this time, the Looe Sergeant had reached the tunnel exit. An exultant Steward was waiting for them. They had their prize with no losses, not that he cared about any losses. That there were no bodies left behind to identify the attackers was what mattered.

He was not happy to learn that Catherine hadn't been killed, but that was a minor matter which could be rectified later.

The blanket that Lady Eleanor was wrapped in yielded a furious lady. She had a short dagger in hand and managed to knife one of her captors in the stomach. He would die in pain later.

The other guards disarmed her and brought her to her knees.

The Steward spoke up, "Now that wasn't very ladylike, My Lady."

Eleanor's response was not fit for polite company.

"Tsk, tsk, what language? Bind her mouth, Sergeant, then search her for more weapons."

After tying a cloth tightly around Eleanor's mouth, he roughly searched her, finding a two-inch blade hanging low between her breasts.

The captive Lady Eleanor was then taken on the two-day journey to Looes. She was kept bound and watched carefully even when relieving herself. The man she had stabbed died on the second day. This event made her captive's treatment of her even rougher.

The Steward let them do all but rape her. He wanted her in good condition when he had her husband surrender to him. After that, he might pleasure himself with her.

Baron Owen-nap was in a meeting on the second day when two messengers arrived.

They had ridden their horse to a lather. One of the horses would probably die.

The messengers were brought to him immediately with the dire news that his Lady had been seized and taken away.

The baby Catherine was left behind in good health due to the quick thinking of her guard, Janet Farmer.

Troops were searching for any sign of Eleanor's captors, but so far, Sera Farmers people hadn't found any traces.

Only fifty-some years of soldiering kept James calm. He knew what could be done was being done.

James and fifty of his troops were bound for Bodmin within the hour. Not double-timing their march but keeping it up hour after hour. Long into the night, they marched by the light of the moon. Dealing death on every mind.

They made the mine pit late in the night. Resting for a few hours, they were on the move again at dawn's first hint of light. They arrived at Bodmin at the end of the third day. It would normally be considered a five-day trip.

Sara Farmer was waiting for Baron Owennap.

"The raiders knew of a secret entrance to Bodmin Keep. They blocked the way in their escape. It has taken us several days, but we have found the exit to the secret tunnel, along with evidence of violence."

"Take me there."

"Do you need to rest?"

"Not yet. Let me see what was left. Then I must rest."

"Very well, follow me."

Horses had been brought out for them. It was just as well as the young baron probably couldn't have walked much further.

The small, abandoned cottage that concealed the tunnel exit was a short ride and a long walk away. Once there, both dismounted.

A squad of ten guards was protecting the area. Inside the cottage, there was blood on the floor.

Sara Farmer directed his attention to a dagger lying on the floor.

"That is Eleanor's," he exclaimed.

"She must have wounded one of them."

She then pointed to a blanket.

"It appears, My Lady, was brought here in that she attacked one of them when freed. There is a trail of blood leaving here. Scouts are following it. They have a five-day head start, so we cannot catch them. We will know where they went."

James nodded, "We will return to the Keep. I do need the rest. Wake me as soon as we know where they are bound."

Baron Owen-nap slept restlessly through the afternoon and the following night. Upon waking, he felt terrible, as though he had been awake the whole time.

He called Sara Farmer and asked for an update.

"One of the scouts has returned with information. Lady Eleanor is alive with her captors. She wounded one who they took with them, he died on the way, and they left his body in a ditch."

"The other scout is still tracking them and leaving his trail well-marked so we may follow. They were heading towards Looe's."

"Then let us be on our way."

"You must eat first, My Lord."

This formality by Sara Farmer reminded James that he needed to listen to her. He was too worked up to think clearly."

"Very well, let's eat, but be quick about it."

He ate like a ravening wolf.
As he ate, other actions were taking place in Looe's.

The Steward had just brought Lady Eleanor to Baron Looe's.

"Here is the Lady you asked for, My Lord."

"Good, you are dismissed. I will take it from here."

Instead of leaving, the Steward approached the Baron.

"What is this, Steward? You forget your place."

"You have a new place, My Lord."

As the Steward said this, he pulled a dagger and stabbed the Baron to death.

"Your new place is Hell, you old fool."

He turned to his accompanying guards.

"Lock her in a cell, then remove this piece of trash."

"Yes, My Lord Looe."

At that, the new Baron smiled. His plan was working, now to bring Baron Owen-nap to heel.

Lady Eleanor was taken to a cell in the Keep. It was above ground, as there was no dungeon. She could see the soldier's barracks out of her barred window. After she watched for several hours, she determined that there were about forty armsmen in residence.

There was one jailor outside of her cell. The cell itself was a small six-foot by six-foot room. Most men wouldn't have been able to sleep on the filthy pallet.

Her older guard jailor was fat and ugly, to say the least. He stank so bad she could smell him six feet away. His teeth were rotten, and his clothes held the remnants of many meals.

He kept rattling the keys on his belt as he talked, as though he would let her out if she yielded to him.

He kept making lurid suggestions to her. When she had seen as much of the Keep's manpower as she could, she approached the bars.

"I have something for you."

He crossed the few feet to her quickly.

"What?"

"This."

She rammed one of her steel hairpins into his eye as she grabbed his tunic to keep him from falling away from the cell door.

Unlocking the crude lock on the cell, she made her escape. The outer door to her cell room was standing wide open. She knew she had little time.

Anyone passing by would see she was out. There was no place to hide her jailor's body, and she had no time.

Eleanor had observed those passing by her cell all day. The servants carried things from her right and returned empty-handed to the left.

She went left out of her prison room. It was shorty led to a kitchen and workshop. As she entered, there were servants clustered together and talking. The real Baron had just been murdered and replaced by the hated Head Steward.

One of the serving girls gasped as she spotted Lady Eleanor. The others turned to see what was going on.

Eleanor told them, "I need your help."

The servants stood there, not knowing what to do. A rotund woman took charge.

"Girls, she needs to be cleaned and fresh clothes."

As the maids took Eleanor in hand, the cook continued.

"Giles, check on the jail. If there is a body, as I expect, hide it."

Turning to Eleanor, she told her, "The old Baron was a bastard, but he was our bastard. All we ask Lady Eleanor is for you to bring your forces and kill the Steward."

Chapter 19

Eleanor and I had a passionate reunion at Looe for several days. We had found the Barony to be in relatively good shape. Three thousand silvers in its treasury and full grain bins.

Surveying teams had been ordered to the area to lay out better roads. The land wasn't fit for crops but was good grazing for the many cattle in the area.

We knew that baby Catherine was safe and sound, but we missed her, so we started back to Owen-nap. The baby had been taken from Bodmin for her safety when Eleanor was missing.

With Looe, Hilston, and Liskeard being brought into the Barony of the Middle Counties, my resources were spread thin.

I decided to spend my time on making better telescopes so a semaphore system between Keeps could be instituted.

Immediately I saw a way to get a better optical glass at the glass house. The lens failures had been thrown in a bin and left. So, I had those added to a batch of glass being melted.

The higher percentage of cullet or failed glass in a batch, the better the batch for both clarity and defects. They skimmed off the top of the molten glass, which contained contaminates. I then had them remelt the glass three times until nothing rose to the top of the batch.

 The molten glass was poured into molds that had a polished surface. The lens blanks were polished with ever finer rouge after the glass cooled in the molds.

The rouge was made from iron oxide, ground, and sieved as fine as possible. The sieves were fine meshed wire, each one smaller than the last. They were stacked, and the iron oxide was poured into the top sieve.

The sieves were shaken until all the iron oxide was separated by size. Each size, grit, or iron oxide was mixed with tallow to polish the glass blanks. They now could make a true optical quality lens.

Chapter 20

Now that we had a ten-power telescope, we could take a serious look at a semaphore system. A rough guess was that we would need to cover 250 miles. From my knowledge of the terrain, it would require twenty-five towers about ten miles apart.

That was average. We might have several that could be fifteen miles apart and some that were only five miles apart.

The towers would be three stories tall, the signal mast another twenty feet. The flat roof of the top floor would be where the signal men would work from. The roof couldn't be perfectly flat, or water wouldn't run off.

The office where records were kept would be on the third floor. The second floor would be living quarters. The ground floor would contain the kitchen and storage.

There would be a side barn for horses and any livestock they cared to keep. There would be a toilet facility with a septic tank. Since we had concrete, it would be easy to set up a septic field.

At the Monastery, I gave a rough sketch of the semaphore tower to one of the scribes and asked that it be made into a formal set of drawings.

Abbot Luke looked very excited as he came up to me with a fancy-looking piece of parchment in hand.

With a huge grin, he told me, "You may now kiss the ring of your Bishop."

I replied, "You can kiss my nether parts!"

Since I had a huge smile, he took this in good humor.

"So the Archbishop in Tintagel sold you a Bishopric?"

"Yes, My Lord, not only that, this document spells out my specific rights. I can now mint coinage!"

"Wonderful! Get with Thomas Smith and see how ready he is. I suspect he can start casting coins immediately."

"It will be interesting when the coins appear in the marketplace at Tintagel."

"That will not be for a while."

"Why?"

I explained Gresham's law. How bad money drives good money away. Our people would keep the crows over other coinage. Only when there was a real need would they spend the better coins.

"So when our coins appear in Tintagel, they will quickly demand a premium!"

"Yes, and that is when our problems will really start. The Archbishop will be upset that you are minting coins that are better than his, and the King will be mad that our economy is stronger than Tintagel's."

"So war is in our future?"

"I'm afraid so. It won't be until next year at the earliest, but it will happen."

Bishop Luke frowned as he thought about the situation.

"My Lord, you knew this would be the result of me becoming a Bishop."

"I'm afraid so."

"I'm not pleased that you have put us into a position of being attacked without consulting with your advisors."

This change in attitude took me aback. Previously Luke had been one of my biggest supporters without any questions. Well, other than the fact that I might be a witch. Once past that hold-up, he went along with everything.

I told him, "You do realize that anything we do would eventually lead to war. We are too rich of a target to be ignored. That is why I have been pushing to make us stronger in all respects to withstand the coming wars."

"Coming wars, you mean there will be more than one?"

"Yes, after we win the first one, which will probably be against King Geraint in Tintagel, King Ine of Wessex will see us as a good acquisition. After we defeat Ine, it would only make sense to continue and take control of the entire British Isles."

"Even Wales and the Scots?"

"All of them. I'm not certain about the Celts in Ireland."

"Why is that?"

"In my time, the Irish divided over religious issues, and you could never pull them together."

"What religious issues?"

Dang! I have stepped into it now.

"In later years, the Church had so much power that it became corrupt. The bishops would sell indulgences that forgave any sin. You could even purchase them in advance."

"God would not accept such a travesty."

"No, but man would. If you were forgiven for your sin, you wouldn't be tried for it."

"Wouldn't the officials have something to say about that?"

"The all-powerful Church ran its courts and directed the nobility on how to run theirs. It got so bad ordinary priests who didn't agree with this protested, becoming the beginnings of the Protestant Churches."

The bishop looked confused. "Why more than one Church?"

"In your youth, as you trained, did you argue about the Holy Bible and how to interpret it?"

"All novices did that?"

"Can you imagine if they had the freedom to do so? They would have founded their Church with their doctrine."

"That would be crazy. There would be dozens of churches."

"Exactly."

"So, how do we avoid this?"

"I don't know that we can. We must set up a structure where the power between Church and state is balanced. Not allow one to have supremacy."

The bishop sat back. He had been sitting forward in an aggressive position. Now he relaxed.

"I see foreknowledge can be a terrible thing."

"It can be. All I can do is try to avoid the mistakes we made in the future."

That night I talked to Eleanor about my troublesome conversation with the bishop.

"Jim, you have to have patience with him and the others. You have turned their world upside down. What you have done is all for the better, but you can't blame them for being fearful for the future. Remember, this was a peaceful little backwater area, and you are turning it into a power. These people weren't raised to run things, maybe the local area, but not a Kingdom."

I had to chuckle at that.

"Why are you laughing?"

"I'm picturing Bishop Luke as Cardinal of the British Isles reporting to the Pope when he realizes that the Pope is corrupt. What will he do?"

"You are mean!'

"Unfortunately, it could come to pass."

"The Pope could raise armies against us."

"Then you, my dear, would end up as the Empress of Europe."

"What is Europe?"

"The whole of the continent. Actually, if it comes to that, you will end up as the Empress of the World."

"And that makes it time to go to sleep so you can continue your dreams."

And that is what we did.

The next day I sent word to my advisors that I would like a meeting in Owen-nap in seven days. It would take that long to get everyone together.

At the meeting, I made certain everyone understood the ramifications of being legally able to mint coins. That King Geriant would see us as a threat to his power.

Tom Smith asked, "Will there be war soon?"

"I don't think so. Unlike our earlier adversaries, Geraint knows what you have to do to prepare for war. He will probably be spying on us for an invasion next year."

"So what must we do?"

"First, we will spy on him to know what forces he intends to bring with him. The more we can learn about his war plans, the better."

Father Timothy asked, "What is a war plan?"

"The entire effort needed to be successful. Geraint needs to know about our military capabilities to bring a large enough force. A large force will need support, everything from weapons to food to horseshoes. It takes a large amount of planning to move a large force of men."

John Steward added, "He must have knowledge of our road system so he can move his troops quickly without jamming them up."

John Chandler asked, "Won't our better roads make it easier for him?"

I replied, "Yes, they will, John. However, they will work more in our favor than his."

"How so?"

"We will have warning of his approach through the semaphore system being built. We will be able to move our troops faster."

"How can we move our troops faster? We don't have enough horses."

"I have been meaning to introduce a new invention. It is called a bicycle."

I then drew a bicycle on one of the blackboards surrounding our meeting room. It was crude compared to bikes of my time, but it would do the job.

Instead of rubber tires, it had wooden wheels. There were no pedals or chains. The riders would have to push them along with their feet, coast down hills, and walk up the steep parts. They would have a sturdy frame and a full backpack could be strapped behind the rider.

I estimated that a rider could do at least twice the miles of a marching column and arrive in better shape.

Once we had the first bikes, we would run tests on every road between Keeps. Once we knew how far a troop could travel in a day, we would build permanent stops so fortifications, latrines, and mess halls would have to be dug and built. Anything that would enable our troops to arrive in better shape.

"We also need to know the King's invasion route. If we know that, we can plan where to fight the battle to our advantage."

The old Baron Saltash spoke up, "Viscount Owen-Nap. You speak of war as though you know it well. Some of us have heard you talk of some of your warrior past, but it would help if you shared what you have done."

"I agree. All of you need to know my background so you will have faith in what I will be asking."

I started with my desire as a youth to join my country's military. I wanted to attend a special school to learn how to be an officer. Of the wars that I had been in. I didn't pull any punches about how nasty they had been, or why logistics were important leading up to the battle and even during it.

I didn't brag about my medals, but at the same time, I laid it all out factually and completely.

There were many questions along the way. Flying machines and boats that traveled underwater amazed them. When I described the destructive power of atomic and hydrogen bombs, they became silent.

I informed them that I would never build these weapons. You could hear sighs of relief. I left out poison gas, death marches, and concentration camps. Enough was enough.

They were all for launching spy satellites until I told them what all needed to be developed.

As Tom Smith said, "Oh, we will have to leave that until later."

How little they knew of what we would have to do first. I doubted it would be in my lifetime.

That brought up an interesting point. How long would I live? I assumed my normal life span unless an accident or war intervened. Maybe I would live until my original death date. What a terrible thought.

Explaining my background in the military and war took the rest of the day. The next day, we firmed up plans to accelerate our roadbuilding, installing semaphore towers, building bicycles, and spying on Geraint.

I also set up a meeting of my most Senior Sergeants from each Keep. I asked how many armsmen they currently have in place. How many more their District could provide? I wanted to know the number of people who could be drafted without harming the district and how many could be drafted in extreme need.

They were to include females in their counts. The ages could be from sixteen to fifty for the regular draft and any that were physically fit for the extreme draft. At least one parent would be allowed to stay home.

These were grizzled warriors, and they understood what I was asking. When they asked who their officers would be, I told them they would be the officers. I would have a staff to help plan and keep records, but they were fighters and didn't need any untrained sons of the nobility telling them what to do.

I also added, "Untrained sons can be your runners."

Chapter 21

While all the warlike efforts were being implemented, life went on. It would take months to finish the roads so we could quickly move men about. The bicycles would have to undergo several iterations before a usable model was developed. The semaphore stations would go up quicker than I originally thought.

Instead of erecting the buildings, we would put up a tall mast with a crow's nest, much like a sailing ship's mast. The signal arms would rise above that. It would take a lot of rope as guy wires, but it would work until we could complete the buildings.

Scouts and surveyors were sent out to find the most likely invasion routes and identify the best battlefields for our army. If possible, we would make fortifications.

Several spies were sent to Tintagel to establish themselves. They were to take no chances at this point, only observe, not take action. Their reports would be few and infrequent. We were trying to learn about King Geraint and his forces, not act against him.

I was going to see how Tom Smith and his apprentices progressed on the bicycle when I heard an old lady talking to her husband.

"I said I needed to buy some clothes, not to try some moths, you deaf old fool!"

I chuckled at that. As I was chuckling, a horn sounded the changing of the guard at the front gate.

I thought, 'he needs a hearing horn.' I then slapped my forehead. A hearing horn would be good, but the first stethoscopes were hearing horns!

First, I asked the old lady her name and where she lived.

"Philis Farmer, My Lord, we live on the third farm on the right down the Mill Road."

"I will be sending your husband a present with instructions on how to use it. He will hear better."

I left her ogling at me.

I quick stepped my way to Thomas's forge. As I thought he was in his office. This was where he spent most of his time now. He must have fifty or more men working for him now.

He groaned as he looked up and saw me.

"Now, what crazy idea do you have?"

"Thomas, my friend, you malign me! I'm here to show you another way to get rich."

"As I said, what crazy idea do you now have."

Shaking my head, I explained what a hearing horn was and that it could be used to listen to a person's heartbeat and other sounds inside their body.

"Why would you want to listen to someone's body?"

"Lady Agnes could answer that better than I can, but it tells if there are ills inside one like their not heart working right or liquid in their lungs. We call it a stethoscope."

"Well, at least this time, we can easily make it. We have half cups used as the base of a candle holder. At the same time, we have smaller cups that hold the candles. The tube to join them can be used as the body of the horn."

"Do you have any made-up?"

"We just completed a set for your wife."

"Great, please convert them right now. Make up two of the horns."

"Only if you tell Lady Eleanor it was at your order."

"Coward!"

"Yep."

People were picking up, 'yep,' from my using it. I was corrupting the English language. Well, it corrupted the language before it became English.

"I will tell her."

"Thank you, she can be biting at times."

I didn't say when I would tell her. He was right. Her tongue could be sharp.

It didn't take Tom long to tear apart the new candlestick holders. It was a shame. The support, our tube, had been engraved with the most beautiful vines.

"Thanks, for doing this, Tom."

"No problem, it got me out of that darn office. Seems that is all I do anymore. I want to be able to hit things sometimes."

"I hear you."

Yes, I was destroying the language.

"Now, remember you are to tell Lady Eleanor this was your idea and that you commanded me to do this."

"I will do that."

I finished that sentence in my head, 'When hell freezes over.'

I had seen her fret over the design for several days.

With two made horns in hand, I left the forge. I was fortunate the Farmers were still shopping. I knew it was them because I heard, "I said to buy a duck!" before I saw them.

I wondered what rhymed with duck. I wasn't about to ask.

I handed Mr. Farmer the horn and showed him how to hold it in his ear. His wife shouted to him, "What does that do?"

He returned it to me and said, "My life is better without listening to her."

They moved on while I stood there shaking my head. Try to do a good deed.

I moved to our new hospital, where Lady Agnes had her office. I don't know when or how she became a Lady, but everyone called her that. Who was I to question it?

I found her in her office. Unfortunately, she was not alone.

"Eleanor, what a surprise to find you here."

I'm dead meat.

"James, it is nice to see you also. What are those things you are bringing to Lady Agnes?"

"These are devices to amplify sound. A deaf man can hear better with one, and the other use is to listen to the sounds inside of a person."

Lady Agnes asked, "How do they work."

I held one to her ear and told her to point it at me. As I spoke, they nodded.

"It does make sounds louder if you point it at the source."

No dummy here, she continued. "it works like that constricting effect that made things move faster."

"Exactly. Now put it against my chest and listen to my heartbeat."

She did and was amazed.

I said, "if a child has fluid in their lungs, you can tell it much easier."

Eleanor had taken the other one from my hand. She tried the hearing test, then held it to my chest.

"I'm glad these worked so well, so I don't have to kill you."

She said while pointing to the vine design on the tube.

"Er, I can explain that."

"Husband, be quiet; it is not good to lie."

"Yes, dear."

Lady Agnes saved me by speaking up.

"This hearing horn will work wonders for Philis Farmer's husband."

"I'm sure it will. See Thomas if you want any more made. I have to be going."

I was glad to escape. Knowing Eleanor, I hadn't heard the end of this. All I can say is that it sounded like a good idea then. At least I didn't ask anyone to hold my beer.

At dinner later, Eleanor was all sweetness and light, making me dread the evening more. When we retired to our rooms that night, she turned on me.

"That was a wonderful idea you had, James. It is amazing what the insides of a human body sound like. The heart beating, the stomach gurgling, the gases moving in the bowels. I'm certain it will help our nurses."

I waited for the other shoe to drop, and I waited as she continued on about how amazing the tubes were. I finally couldn't stand it anymore.

"I'm sorry about your candlesticks. I was hurrying to make the horns, and there they were. I know you spent a lot of time on the design."

"Fiddle-faddle, Tom can always make me more candlesticks. The stethoscope is an important invention."

"Thank you. I know we can improve it when we get an elastic material."

"You mean something that stretches?"

"Yes."

"Like dandelion sap after it hardens. We used to collect it as kids and make small balls which we could bounce."

This information was all news to me!

"It is simple: collect dandelion roots, leaves, and flower stems, crush them, and squeeze out the milky sap. It also works with milkweed and morning glories."

I grabbed Eleanor in a hug and kissed her.

"This is wonderful. There are many things we can do with rubber! Now excuse me for a minute to see if I can find anything in my library."

I started looking at the titles. I had seen in the many libraries I had visited. It is a shame that I don't have a built-in index or even a search feature. All I could do was first picture the library and then its various sections. When I had a section visualized, I read the titles, hoping to find one on rubber.

I finally came across a book. I had leafed through that information on using sap or latex to make a useable rubber item. The sap had to be rinsed and cleaned in warm water to remove impurities. The mixture is left to settle, and the rubber is skimmed off.

It would help to add morning glory sap, as the mixture would produce a better rubber.

Once you have cleaned the rubber, you can make objects with it. Once the object is formed, you vulcanize it to set the rubber. The finished product will be stable. It is serviceable and will not wear as well as latex collected from rubber trees.

To make a conveyor belt or any flat surface, pass the latex with sulfur added between two rollers to get the thickness you want. Trim knives control the width. The last step is to vulcanize. That is simply passing the new rubber strip between two rollers heated by steam through tubes inside the rollers. This step cures the rubber.

To make a solid configuration such as a plug, put the latex/sulfur mixture inside a mold and heat it until vulcanization occurs. Voila, you have a finished piece in the shape needed.

A rubber tube pushes the latex/sulfur mixture through a tube with a core in its center. The extruded tube would then be passed through a steam bath for vulcanization.

Making rubber parts sounds simple, but what temperatures do you use for the vulcanization steps? How much sulfur is needed?

I suspected experimenting would take a year or more to work things out.

Still, this was an important step. Now, the question was how much latex dandelions produce. We would need a more dependable source.

I explained all this to Eleanor and some of the important uses of rubber parts. She got the idea that a flexible part would have many uses. For fun, I told her how latex was woven into fabrics to make a stretchable waistline. She wanted to start on that first thing in the morning.

I had to remind her that winter was coming and that no dandelions would be available.

I then changed the subject to calm her down.

"We discussed going to London to see what markets are available there. We have put it off so long that our products are on the market there. I would like to see how they are being sold and get ideas for new ones."

"What about this coming war with King Geraint."

"The earliest he could move his army is in the spring, and I doubt he will move that fast. It will probably be after the fall harvest."

"Then we have time. I wonder if there are many shops in London."

"The only way to find out is to go look. Well, you could ask people who have been there."

"The only people who have been there are sailors, and they are all men. They wouldn't know shopping."

Trying to defend sailors as being knowledgeable about shopping would be a losing battle.

"What about your father? He has been there."

"He is still a man."

At that, I shut up and started more pleasurable activities.

Chapter 22

You would think that a trip would be easy. When I was single, I would throw some clothes in a suitcase or bag and take off. Being married made it a logistical nightmare.

The first issue was whether we should take baby Catherine with us. If we did, the nurse would have to accompany us, plus her bodyguard. After discussion, we decided, based on the kidnapping, that one bodyguard wouldn't be enough. So maybe we should leave the baby at home.

Leaving her at home had its issues. Would there be attempts to take her or kill her? Shortly after the kidnapping, we took several measures. First, the interior of the Keep had wooden and plaster walls. That made for comfortable rooms. However, we needed a safe room for us and our child.

Concrete walls reinforced with rebar were installed around our bedroom suite. The door had a steel backing installed with two bars that could be used to block the door. The door had six hinges instead of the standard three to resist a battering ram.

The ceiling was reinforced from above. We were on the top floor, so the flat roof, which served as an observation platform, was already concrete and rebar to resist catapults.

The suite consisted of a bedroom, bathroom, sitting room, a small kitchen, and a dining area. It was self-contained. A cupboard contained a month's food supply. Water was available in the bathroom. The smoke from the kitchen fire was vented through a very small, concealed pipe exiting the side of the building. It would only be used at night.

Unlike many other rooms in the house, there were no windows. I don't know how we could make it any more secure.

One potential weakness was the people involved. I introduced a new concept. A background check was run on everyone who had access to our suite. The criteria were no relatives from other Baronies in the last two generations. Since people didn't travel much, only one guard didn't pass the check.

I promoted him to a better position in one of the other Districts. That way, there was no stigma attached to the move.

After several days of waffling on what to do, Eleanor and I decided to leave Baby Catherine at home. If anything happened to us on the trip, Eleanor's father would be Catherine's regent, and if he passed, it would be John Steward. Followed by a council made up of Father Timothy, Thomas Smith, and Lady Agnes.

This line of succession of regents was formalized in a document signed by all of us. Each had a personal copy.

This plan may have seemed excessive, but one never knew how a journey might unfold. Also, the document was good even after we returned home. It secured Catherine's position.

The trip became easier to plan after that. I packed my clothes in one bag and was ready to go. We needed a wagon to haul Eleanor's bags to Saltash.

Upon arriving at Saltash, I spent two days with John Chandler, getting up to date on what our trade missions to London had accomplished. From the money that had been sent back, I knew we were doing very well. We were ahead of our projected sales.

John wanted to know if we could increase the production of reading stones, eyeglass lenses, and frames. The new farming implements were not doing as well as we had hoped. The farmers were very conservative and would wait several years to see how our demonstration fields would turn out.

Telescopes and microscopes were selling like hotcakes. John had the prices raised twice because of the demand. They were now up to a thousand silver each. We would ship them to London in lots of five, and they would be sold before arrival. There was a waiting list for telescopes.

Both the microscope and telescopes we were now making were far better than the originals. They were so much better that I ordered that we take the originals back in trade, allowing a ninety percent discount on the new models. Our merchants screamed at that, but what could they do? I controlled the franchises.

We would also be taking copies of Bishop Luke's recent book. I had dictated a basic textbook on double-entry bookkeeping. It made theft harder and left a clearer picture of the financial situation. My accounts were tracked with this method.

We had no shortage of funds, but this would enable us to plan, especially on major projects such as road building and the semaphore towers. It also allowed us to have a reasonable military budget.

Our crossbowmen had been beefed up to two hundred trained fighters, with another one hundred spearmen to protect the crossbow teams.

The team would have three crossbows. One was loaded while the other was fired. The third would be a spare if one of the primary bows failed.

The bows didn't fail often, but they did fail. Each team had a crossbowman or woman, a loader, and someone who brought up additional bolts, water, and food.

They would relieve the other two people as needed. It was tiring holding a heavy crossbow, even though the bows had a support rod.

The rate of fire was a round every ten seconds or six rounds a minute. With two hundred bows in action, this meant there were 1200 bolts launched every minute. It would take an enormous army to charge into that.

There was a shortage of horses, so we couldn't have a cavalry.

My army would be considered a field army that could also defend. What they weren't set up for was a siege. But I was working on that.

I felt comfortable enough that a trip to London for several weeks would be no problem.

The ship we would be sailing on was a single mast, carvel-built hull with a rear rudder. The hull and rudder were considered risky innovations, but I knew they would become the standard of the sailing world.

I was told it might take a week to get to London, depending on the wind and tides. In my day, it would be an easy eight hours.

The Compass Rose, owned by John Chandler, was in excellent shape. Eleanor and I, no other passengers, were welcomed aboard by the captain. I never learned his name. He was Captain to all.

Our cabin was small but not cramped. It had two small bunks built into the sides with a short rail around them so one wouldn't fall out in rough seas. We ate in the captain's cabin.

The trip itself was pleasant. The weather cooperated, and we had smooth sailing. Late on day three, we entered the mouth of the Thames. Eleanor and I thought we were in London when we made the Thames.

But once in the river way, the winds became a problem. The crew worked hard as they tacked back and forth across the river to make any headway. It took us another two days to fight our way upriver.

The river was clogged with ships. They were in all sizes, from an ancient coracle to ships larger than ours. Ours was the only one with a stern rudder.

The river itself wasn't that pleasant. We would come upon masses of feces floating downstream. I knew that this would get worse every year for centuries to come unless major changes were implemented. As it was, I wouldn't eat any fish from that river.

Children were playing on the river, too. They had made small rafts and were paddling them around the banks of both shores. One raft came across our bow. I don't know how we didn't hit it. I heard the kids yelling at each other.

"Ernie, steer to the right," yelled a dark-haired girl.

Her hair was so black it seemed to have a purple sheen.

"Peg, I will steer any bloody way I want," he retorted.

I didn't hear her response as we sailed upstream without running them down.

There were many small villages along the way. Everyone had a dock. The largest of them, Greys, looked very prosperous.

We finally reached London and docked where Big Ben would stand. The city, really a town at most, was tired and rundown. It had seen better days under Roman occupation. None of the buildings or bridges I associated with London existed.

We were met at the dock by one of John Chandler's people. Our ship had been spotted coming upstream, and a rider was sent to inform him of our arrival. Peter Finch was to be our guide for our stay.

He arranged for our baggage to be loaded on a wagon and had horses for Eleanor and me to ride. Peter told us that he knew most of the Inns in London and wouldn't want us to stay at any flea and lice-infested places.

We were to stay at a house used by John Chandler's people on their various missions. It had been upgraded to our standards of cleanliness, which meant we had clean water and waste removal.

Riding the muddy streets was revolting at best. How anyone could live like this, I couldn't fathom. Besides rats roaming in the daylight, the occasional dead dog rotted in place.

I asked Peter, "Is all of London like this?"

"Most of it, the center is kept clean. That is where ours and other shops are."

This was good news to Eleanor as she had been looking more and more out of sorts as we rode to the house.

The house itself was inside a walled compound. The gates were closed on our arrival but opened quickly. It was like riding into a different world. A clean world. This house was bigger than those in Owen-nap but would have fitted in.

A huge cistern gathered the water for the house. There was a septic system for human waste. All in all, it was a slice of home. That thought made me stop for a moment. Since when had I been thinking of Owen-nap as home?

We were given use of what was called the owner's suite. It had a bathroom, bedroom, living room, and dining room. It was furnished very nicely. I could see the Chandler team in London lived well.

Since it was late in the evening, we asked for a light meal in our room. It only took a few minutes for a repast of meats and cheeses to be laid out for us. It turned out our suite also had two attendants who cooked and took care of our wardrobe.

After eating, we each took a bath and fell into bed. Unusual for us, we went straight to sleep.

Awake at daylight, we made up for our negligence of the past evening.

After our morning ablutions, we dressed and went downstairs to see what we could find to eat.

People were at the dining room table eating food laid out on a sideboard. It was self-serve. I took ham, eggs, and a bowl of ever-present porridge. I was beginning to like the stuff.

Peter came in just as we were finishing. We discussed our plans for the day. Of course, Eleanor wanted to shop, and I wanted to visit our shops. We both could accomplish our goals as all the better stores were in one area of London.

Peter gave us a choice of riding or a carriage. Eleanor decided we would have a carriage since it could carry our purchases. I thought we might have a wagon follow behind, but I shut my mouth.

The area where the stores were was in what I remembered as the Kensington area, sitting where the distant future Harrods would be.

Chapter 23

The carriage ride was miserable. There were no springs, so it bounced and lurched through the countless potholes of London. That is until it reached the shopping area. There the streets were built by the Romans to last.

During the coach ride, I went over the instructions I had given to John Chandler's agent. If Eleanor and I were invited to meet the Emperor, I would go alone and tell them she wasn't feeling well. In the meantime, she and her maids were to go aboard the ship and stay there.

If guards came to collect me and take me to the Emperor, I would use the code word 'omega,' and we would assume the worst. In this case, certain actions would be taken immediately. It meant the leaders in London were going to take us hostage.

They were to get Eleanor safely aboard the ship at once. Then they were to pull all our merchandise and funds from the stores and load them on the ship. Any personnel who wanted to leave were free to join us. The ship would be crowded, but we would all fit.

I also asked where I would be taken if held hostage.

Peter replied, "It would take the self-styled Emperor to hold you hostage. He would hold you in the Ambassadors' suites in his Palace if he didn't want to destroy you. Those rooms are designed to keep the Ambassadors and their entourage from leaving them.

"If he means you ill, you will be held in his prison cells."

I asked, "are his people as corrupt as you say?"

"I don't know how they could be any more corrupt than they are."

"Good, here is what I want you to do."

I may not be taken hostage. If taken, I may not be held in either of those two locations. Then I was depending on dishonest people staying bought. Still, it was worth the silver as insurance. When I told Peter what I wanted, he laughed. He thought it would work well.

The stores themselves were a mishmash of old and new. New didn't mean better. Some of the old ones were well-built, while some of the new ones looked like they would collapse anytime.

The two ladies assigned to our suite accompanied Eleanor while she shopped. While I would visit our stores to see what they looked like and how they were doing.

The first shopping day went well, at least from the number of packages Eleanor had delivered to the ship. I think she was trying to buy out every store in London. Being an intelligent man, I didn't ask my wife how much was spent. I asked if she was happy with her purchases.

She told me she had found some of what she wanted and hoped to find the rest on the morrow.

"If needed, dear, we could stay a third day."

"Thank you, but I will have visited all the stores by tomorrow afternoon. If they don't have what I need, we could go to Armorica."

"Where in Armorica? I'm not familiar with their cities."

"I think Vellooasses is the biggest port. Venti and Osismil are also busy ports, so any of them should have good shops or at least a marketplace."

Peter spoke up, "We trade mostly in Vellooasses. It has access to both the Frankish and Roman trade routes."

"How long of a journey is it from Saltash?"

"In the summer, it is an easy two-day trip. Winter storms will make it five days if you arrive at all."

"Let's plan on a trip next summer."

Eleanor replied, "That sounds good to me."

I didn't tell Eleanor that I thought we would be in a war by late spring. Sufficient unto the day is the evil thereof.

The first shop selling our wares was the Button Shop. This place was mint. It had been put together by Lady Agnes and her crew, using their profits for children's programs. One of their programs was for orphans.

The kids were running wild in the city, stealing to survive. The city was glad to get rid of them, and we were glad to have them.

The city watch would bring orphans to the collection point as they captured them. The collection point was set up like a barracks. The kids would be cleaned up, clothed, and fed. Some of the older children had led such hard lives they weren't redeemable. Not in the sense of joining our society.

These children were immediately put into our army, where we hoped discipline would bring them around. Undoubtedly, we would have to hang some of them.

There were over fifty children ready to sail with us from London to Owen-nap. Once in Owen-nap, they would undergo a health check, get new clothes, and start school, as most wouldn't be able to read and write.

Once the child was educated, they would be tested and interviewed to see which direction they would like to take. This program was building for the future. We needed all the manpower we could get, and I supported any shortfalls in financing they had, but so far, it was self-supporting.

One would think a store selling buttons wouldn't have enough business to survive. But the store had a line of women waiting to get in. Once we could edge around the line, with many snide comments about men looking at women's stuff, I saw why they were waiting.

There were buttons of all sizes and colors. In this day and age, it normally costs a fortune to have something fancy made. These buttons were reasonably priced and would dress up any outfit.

There weren't only buttons. There were brooches, necklaces, bracelets, and rings. A line of combs caught my eye. Some were the traditional combs men carried in my day, but there were Spanish-type combs for raised hairstyles.

Besides plastic items, there were bobby pins on display, with young ladies demonstrating how they were used.

There was a cosmetic counter selling face paints, rouges, lipsticks, eyeliners, mascaras, and hair coloring one would expect. These products were all for sale locally. The only thing different about ours was they were safe. We did animal and human testing before we let products on the market.

Some chemicals used locally contained arsenic, lead, and other undesirable elements. While we didn't have long-term results, we knew that our products didn't contain any of the bad stuff and had been tested for short-term problems.

The women buyers in the store were handing over silver like it was worthless. They had to have our products. I asked the store manager how much silver they were taking in daily. She told me they were averaging eight hundred silver a day and had some days reached two thousand silver.

I whistled at that amount.

"Where do you keep the silver?"

"Guards pick up the daily take and escort it to the vault building."

"Where is that?"

"I'm not sure, as I've never been there. I think it is near the warehouse and visitors compound."

"Are we treating you and your employees fairly?"

"We are on a profit-sharing plan. We are all making more than we ever dreamed of. If you now will excuse me, I have to start the next fashion show."

I had to stay and see what that was all about. There was a hall next door that was set up like a Paris salon from my time. It had a walkway and chairs surrounding it, and a bar with refreshments set up in the back.

The models were young wives or daughters of the local nobility. One young lady was exceptionally attractive, and the local term for her translated into super-model.

She was the daughter of one of the smaller Baronies outside of London. Word was that she would marry at least a Duke's son, if not better.

Some things don't change.

There were even several reporters there from their daily broadsheet. These were one-page, one-story newsletters sold on the streets by hawkers.

I suggested to the store manager that she hire some of the models who were all working for free as an ego trip and put on some private shows of the better merchandise.

One thing they needed to add to the product line was mirrors. We had brought the first ones available with us. They would make a fantastic kickoff item for their first private showing.

I had a small mirror in my pouch, so I took her aside and showed her. She didn't want to give it back to me.

"How many of these do you have?"

"We brought five hundred mirrors, most that size, but some are floor mounted to show the whole body at once."

"The little ones will sell for hundreds, the larger for thousands. When can we put them on sale?"

"If all goes well here, as soon as you can set up a show."

"I will start putting together a list of invitees."

"I have a suggestion about the broadsheet people."

"What is that?'

"Don't invite any of them, but have one of your doormen accept bribes to let several of them in. They will push the story harder since they will have a 'scoop'. The ones that didn't get in will try to get more information to get back in the game. The result will be more publicity than you ever have had."

"My Lord, you are a genius!"

I smiled and nodded, not really, just a survivor of twenty-first-century advertising and marketing ploys.

On my next trip, I will talk about free samples.

After the Button Shop, we stopped at the bookshop. They sold books, pamphlets, and newspapers from Owen-nap.

It also was doing a booming business. Like the Button Shop, they had many more items for sale than the name implied. There was a true coffee shop set up. Like the Button Shop, there was a line waiting to get in. The only difference was that they were all men.

Except for the clothing, it reminded me of what an eighteenth-century English coffee house must have looked like. There were ship captains, local businessmen, several men in togas, and one dressed as a Viking.

I don't think central casting could have done any better.

There was a section selling writing paper and pens. They even had one of our new fountain pens on display. It was in a locked glass-topped case. It was one of our more decorated ones, and he was asking a thousand silver for it. There were plain ones for sale at one hundred silver each.

"How much are you taking in daily?"

"A little over one thousand silver a day, My Lord. One day we made almost five thousand silver."

"Where are you keeping all this silver?"

"It is picked up by guards and taken to the vault in the warehouse compound."

I could see that a problem was building here. I would have to check into a few more things.

"What all are you doing to create sales."

"We have an hourly reading of the stories printed in the Owen-nap newspaper. We read the same story eight times during the day. This encourages customers to turn over the tables in the coffee shop. There now are regulars at each hourly reading. Some early before their work, some at lunch, or dinner. Many just leave work and come here.

"My Lord, would you like to see our latest project?"

Interesting how the men use My Lord more often than the women.

"Certainly."

He took me to the shop next door, which wasn't open for business. Inside some workmen were in the process of assembling a printing press.

"We intend to have a London newspaper starting next week."

"Does the local government know about this?"

"Yes, we had to obtain a separate business license. They have insisted on having a censor on site to make certain we don't malign any officials or question policy."

"Good, I'm not ready to go to war with them."

"You say that like you may someday."

"You never know."

Chapter 24

I had coffee at the coffee shop but was getting hungry. Peter took me to an individually run shop. It was serving foods that I had introduced to the Owen-nap kitchens.

I had a hamburger and fries with ale. I hadn't gotten around to introducing carbonated beverages yet. I would have loved to have a Coke.

After our late lunch, we headed back to the compound. I had some serious follow-up questions as to our procedures.

"Peter, when we return, I want to see the vault."

"Yes, My Lord, it isn't a vault but a strong room inside the warehouse."

"How is it guarded?"

"There are guards at the warehouse door night and day."

"What about patrolling guards?"

"We haven't found them to be necessary."

"Do you know how much silver and gold are in this strongroom?"

"Not really, but it must be a huge amount."

What did Willie Sutton say? "I robbed banks because that was where the money was."

I know he claimed he never said it, but it was true. The money was in our warehouse, so that is where the thieves will be. The only reason we hadn't been hit yet was that no one had put together how much we had.

"Peter, who is in charge of the vault?"

"I guess the warehouse manager."

"Let's find him."

Peter led me to the manager's office, where he was closing up for the day. I was introduced to Andrew Carter.

"Andrew, do you know how much is in the strongroom?"

"No, I can find out quickly, though. We keep a set of books inside the strongroom. Whenever money is deposited, it is recorded as to date, amount, and source."

The strong room had stout-looking walls and was in the center of the building. At least no one could access it by breaking into a back wall.

The door was standing open.

"Why isn't the door locked and barred closed?"

"It is more convenient to open it all day so we can access it at need."

I kept my counsel at this point.

"May I see the accounting book you have to refer to?"

"Certainly, My Lord."

The book was open on a table.

"How does this work?"

"The guards escort each shopkeeper here. They enter the amount being deposited and leave the silver on one of the racks."

"Does anyone count the silver being brought in?"

"No, My Lord."

I had seen the silver being loaded onto a wagon at the Book Shop, my last stop of the day. The silver was taken in bags and placed in the wagon. No one had counted the amount being deposited.

I think I had honest people working for me, but this amount of money and how easy it would be to steal it would tempt anyone.

"There are going to be changes in our system. I need a meeting with you and our shopkeepers before starting their business.

"Where at?"

The Book Shop so we can have coffee."

"I will take care of it, My Lord."

I brought Eleanor up to date on my findings of the day.

"So the safety of all our earnings is your main concern?"

"No, dear, the real concern is that we are being too successful."

"How do you mean?"

"We are taking too much silver out of London's economy. They are in danger of being taken over by the Angles of Mercia. They need the silver to pay their fighting men. We are taking so much that there will be problems."

"What can we do?"

"We have to decide to become an ally or reduce our presence. We are a disabling influence, and the emperor here can't let this stand. He will have to ban us or conquer us.

"Another way is to figure out how to spend most of the silver here."

"What could we buy? They don't seem to have anything that we need. The city is dirty, and the people don't live as well. All they have is an excess of mouths."

"Eleanor, you are a genius!"

"What do you mean?"

"Your statement of excess mouths is the answer. I will gain an audience with the emperor and attempt to hire soldiers, farmers, and everyone we need.

"We need people. They need silver."

Eleanor replied, "Now that I have solved our problems, let's go to bed."

"First, I need to get the silver on the ship. And then, yes, dear."

I ordered all the silver in the warehouse to be loaded into two wagons which had bags of saltpeter and sulfur loaded on top. At the break of the day, they would be sent to the ship for loading.

The next morning, I made sure Eleanor, and her maids were safely on the ship, then sent a message to the Palace. I asked for the ruler. I refused to call him Emperor, at least in my mind, if I could have an audience.

I had word sent to all the shopkeepers that things may go south, and they and their staff should be ready to evacuate at a moment's notice.

Things were to look normal on the surface until they weren't. When the ship was fully loaded, it would be crowded, but there would be enough room.

Word came back from the Palace that the emperor would give me an audience after lunch. This meant I wasn't in high favor as I should have been invited for a meal.

The plan was if I didn't come out of the Palace in three hours, the ship would set sail. The timing was chosen to coincide with the outgoing tide.

I spent the morning at our experimental farm outside of the city with our manager John Farmer. As a former farm boy, it looked good to me. Neat buildings and fences and crops in the field looked like they were doing well.

There was a demonstration field with plows, seed drills, a harrow, and even a new combine based on the Gallic Reaper.

The Gallic Reaper had been in use until about 300 A.D. by the Romans. It had disappeared sometime in the last five hundred years.

The original Gallic Reaper had a comb at the front to collect grain heads. An operator would knock the heads into a tray for collection. We added a stripper based on an Australian design with a comb at the front and a mechanical beater to knock the heads off the grain.

There was also a cutter bar and elevator to move the heads into a storage bin for later threshing. We would introduce a winnower to thresh the grain from the heads in later models. We didn't want to introduce too much change and complications at once.

I interviewed the experimental farm manager.

"How is it going? Are the locals adopting any of this?"

"We have many farmers come to check us out and even make return trips with other farmers. They are a conservative bunch, though, and are slow to change. I can't blame them. They will starve if they make a wrong decision. I suspect they will become more interested when they see the equipment in action after a full growing season."

"We may not have the chance to demonstrate the equipment.

I explained what had happened to the local ruler and that we may have to flee.

"How will I know to leave? And what do we do with the equipment?"

"Everything here will be safe for a day. Come back to town with me."

"What about my family?"

"Bring them with you."

"My wife won't be happy about leaving her things."

"Will her treasures fit in one wagon?"

"Yes, My Lord."

"Then load it all up. Anything that you have to leave behind, I will replace it. Better yet, can you replace your belongings if I give you five hundred silvers?"

"For five hundred silvers, I would replace my wife."

"Really?"

"No, not really, but that is a lot of money. What about the equipment if we don't return."

"Do you have a helper that could take over? We are demonstrating things here, not selling them. The only reason we are doing this is to relieve the chance of starvation."

"I have a helper who knows as much about this as I do."

"Good, we will leave him one hundred silver to live on and continue the demonstrations."

"You are generous, My Lord."

"If you only knew."

I left John to break the news to his wife. I hoped they would move fast and make it in time.

By the time we got back to the city, it was time for me to go to the Palace. I had two guards and Peter as my escort. They wouldn't be allowed in with me. That was fine. They were to wait outside, and if I didn't arrive on time, head to the ship and cast off.

I had to shake my head at what was being called the Palace. It was a small keep on a hill. The so-called emperor claimed his authority from Rome, but the Romans hadn't had a presence here for over two hundred years.

Today, London was in a tug-of-war between Wessex and Mercia. In my history, Merica, under Alfred the Great, would conquer all. This time, things would be different.

Not that I hated the Angles. They and the Saxons that lived here would be a strong combination until they were conquered by the Frankish Normans.

I probably remembered it wrong, but I didn't care enough to look it up. My problem was that Cornwall and the Britons, now my people, would be marginalized.

We would be walled off and held back until conquered many years later. But I wouldn't let that happen. Not that I wanted to be the ruler of the British Isles. It was a case of growing or dying. I agree with General Patton on the subject. Let some other SOB die for his country.

I wasn't given the warmest welcome at the Palace. First, I was given a quick search. It was too quick. Next, I had to wait forty-five minutes for my audience to show me how unimportant I was.

A Steward told me how I had to walk in, bow down, and then go to my knees to show that I understood how great of a man the Emperor was.

My first thought was, 'hell no.' On second thought, I decided to play his game and not give him a reason to try to imprison me.

When the door opened, I was practically shoved through like a prisoner being hailed in front of a judge. I kept my balance and my temper.

Walking forward, I bowed, then went to both knees. This gave me time to look at the man demanding this. I think he was a man.

He wore kohl makeup around his eyes, and his cheeks were rouged. He was fat, and his hair was greasy. It hadn't been washed in years.

I wondered if I was going to give this clown any more strikes.

"So, you wish to speak to me? How much tribute have you brought."

Strike three, or maybe we were up to seven about now.

"None."

"Then I have no use for you. I understand your businesses have been doing very well. I have sent my soldiers to close them down and seize all your money. You will be held for ransom. Take him away."

I thanked the Lord for the steps I had taken.

The guards roughly pushed me in front of them to a hallway and then down the steps to what I thought was his dungeon.

I was shoved into a cell, and the jailor locked the door. The cell was about seven-foot square, just large enough to lie down. Not that I would, as the bed of straw looked like it had been there for years. There was a bucket in the corner for my waste.

I turned to the jailor.

"Have my people spoken to you?"

"Yes, they have."

Chapter 25

"However, the fifty silver they gave me was not enough. I need another one hundred to take you to the exercise yard."

"I thought that might be the case."

I showed the jailor two pouches. Each had fifty silvers.

"One now and the other when we are in the yard."

He opened the cell door and grabbed the bag. He led me up another set of stairs to an enclosed courtyard.

An eight-foot wall surrounded the courtyard. I was to cause a bruise on the jailor and climb over the wall. What wasn't as described was the armed guard waiting.

The jailor held his hand, "Give me the other pouch, and you won't get a beating."

I had nothing to lose at this point, so I held out the pouch with my left hand. When he reached, I stabbed him in the stomach with the dagger I had up my sleeve.

Police work 101, when searching, do it thoroughly.

The guard was slow in reacting as he started to pull his sword. I hit him with the butt of my dagger, breaking his nose. As his hands went to his face, I kneed him and brought the butt of the dagger down on his head, knocking him out cold. It may have killed him. I didn't stop to check.

I took a running leap at the wall and caught the top. Looking over the wall carefully, I saw it faced an alley. I lifted myself to the top of the wall and went over the side into the alley.

Peter spoke up, "My Lord, are you okay?"

"Yes, but we have to move quickly."

Peter had brought a cloak with a hood to help hide me. We went to the ship, walking like we had a place to go, but not in a hurry.

When we arrived at the ship, I was pleased that John Farmer, his wife, and his two small children were boarding. They had traveled light as all they brought fit in three bags.

The captain had seen me coming and ordered me to cast off as soon as we were aboard. The tide had started to ebb back to the ocean, so we made good progress downstream.

Sails set, with the wind at our back, we were on a long reach downstream. I hoped that Peg and Ernie weren't playing on the river today because they wouldn't have a chance to get out of our way.

They weren't, so they would live to play another day. All went well until we made Dover and turned to the west. The sea and winds were in our favor on the way from Saltash, but now they were against us.

One day from London to Dover, then four days of tacking back and forth to reach Saltash. They were a miserable four days. The ship was overcrowded with fifty orphans on board, and all fifty were seasick. The ship reeked after two days. By the time we reached Saltash, most of the passengers had been throwing up.

One exciting thing happened on the way to Saltash. One of the town passengers was watching most of the passengers leaning over the side rail, throwing up.

He exclaimed, "What a shemozzle."

I walked up to him and said, "Borekh habo."

He turned quickly to me. " Ver bistu?"

I laughed and held up my hands. "I'm afraid I just used all the Yiddish I know, and I agree it is chaos."

"Frank Goldman." He held out his hand to shake mine.

"James Owen-nap." I took his dry, firm hand in mine. We shook hands as we looked each other over.

"I didn't know we had any Jewish people on board."

235

He asked, "Is that a problem?"

"Not with me. I'm just a little surprised. I didn't know any of your faith was in London."

"Only me and my family."

"How many of you are there?"

"My wife Miriam, son Jakob, and our daughter Heddy. They are thirteen and fifteen, with Jakob being the elder."

"May I ask what you were doing in London?"

Frank got a pensive look. "Could we speak in private, My Lord."

"I'm not your Lord, and I get enough of that every day, call me Jim or James. Let's go to my cabin. Oh, my wife will be there. Do you want to invite yours?"

"Normally, yes, but she is busy." He gestured to the rails.

We adjourned to my cabin. After I introduced Frank to Eleanor, he didn't mess around.

"I'm a scout for our community. We are hunting for a safe place for us."

"Who is us?"

"The Jewish business communities in Rome and Constantinople."

"That's a large number of people, would all move to this safe place?"

"Oh no, we would continue to live and do business in those cities. We would flee if the Christians decided we were the devil's spawn. They do this every fifty years or so. We want a place to go when this comes to pass."

I thought this to be a pragmatic approach to life, but it was still foreign to me. I had read about it, but to hear one who had lived it was sad.

"What about in between?"

"That is where we have a lot to offer to have a safe haven."

Eleanor spoke up. "Such as?"

"As you can imagine, our community has a lot of money. We lend most of it out, but we keep a large reserve so when things go bad, we can recover. We need a place to keep it safe. I thought London might be it, but not now."

Eleanor asked, "Why not now."

"Because you have destroyed their economy, Wessex will take them over soon. Wessex is as greedy as London, so that is not the place for us."

I asked, "Why do you say I destroyed their economy."

"It is no secret that you sold many products in London and now have taken your profits. I estimate you have over seventy-five thousand silvers of the three hundred thousand that made up their economy."

"It is more like one hundred and twenty-five thousand silvers."

"Their economy will grind to a halt without enough money to exchange. As I have said, you have destroyed them, and Wessex will now attack."

"That is what Eleanor and I thought. What are your plans now?"

"To see if Owen-nap is a possible site. If not, look across the Celtic Sea."

"We may be able to work things out, but first, I will have to have a long conversation with our Bishop and the local priest."

"Good. If they are not accepting, then it won't work."

We didn't meet his seasick family until we reached Saltash several days later. Eleanor and I invited them to stay at his Keep with Baron Saltash's permission. While recovering from their trip, Eleanor and I rode to Owen-nap.

The work crews had finished the road between the two towns, and our coach had sprung, so it wasn't the torture that it had been. I wanted to ride horseback but was informed by Sara Farmer this was no longer possible.

I would have an escort of forty mounted armsmen on all trips and would be inside the coach for safety. The coach now had light armor protecting the passengers. There were also weapons stored under the seats.

My guards were taking no chances.

When we arrived in Owen-nap, our first order of business was to check on our daughter Catherine. When she saw Eleanor, she held out her chubby little arms and said, "MMMum."

I tried to get her to say "Da-da" but had no luck. She didn't even want me to hold her. It was all mother and "MMMMum."

I acted as though it didn't matter, but I was hurt a little. I knew Catherine would take to me sooner or later, but I wanted her love now.

The next morning, while the girls were still having their love fest, I talked to the bishop. I was lucky that both he and Father Timothy were at a conference.

While ale was being fetched for us, I updated them on my trip.

Bishop Luke said, "It seems like you left them in a fine mess but did well for the Barony. It's what we have come to expect from you."

"Well, there is one more thing. How do the both of you feel about Jews?"

Father Timothy said, "They crucified God's only begotten child."

I replied, "I thought that was the Romans."

"Yes, but it was at the Jewish leader's urgings."

"Why did they want him crucified?"

"Because he was saving the good Jews."

"So there were bad Jewish leaders and good Jewish people?"

"I hadn't thought of it that way, but yes."

I turned to the bishop. "What are your thoughts?"

"Jesus cast the Jewish money lenders out of the Temple."

"Well, since it was a Jewish country, you would expect the money lenders to be Jewish."

The bishop knew well enough to ask, "how many Jews have you brought back with you?"

"A small family of four."

"Are they good Jews?"

"I know they haven't requested anyone to be crucified."

"What is their profession?"

"Money lenders."

That answer had both men standing up.

"Are you mad? Christ threw them out of his Temple."

"Only the Temple. He didn't prevent them from money lending, just not on sacred grounds."

"In the future that you came from, were Jews allowed in your country."

"Yes, they are a minority, but the United States is a live and let live country. The Constitution even protects everyone's right to practice their religion, and not let the government force a religion on anyone."

"Then how does the Holy Church remain in power?"

"They don't. Politics and religion don't mix. Well, the churches may take a political stance, but the government isn't allowed to."

"Then how does the Holy Church save people?"

"By doing good works so that people want to belong."

Father Timothy said, "But people don't know what's good for them. We have to shepherd the flock."

"True once they have joined the flock. Until then, they are free to believe what they want. Even after they join the Church, they may leave.

"Father Timothy, have you ever had anyone try to leave your congregation and go to another, say, Saltash?"

"Not that I know of."

"I'm sure the busybodies of your congregation would let you know."

He had to smile at that. "You are so right. They tell me things I don't want to know, and many times they aren't even true."

"So you must be a good Shepherd. If someone left your Church, would you hunt them down and punish them?"

"No, I might seek them out and try to gain an understanding of why they have left, but punishing them for my failure as a Sheperd, never."

"Then you must be a good Sheperd. None have left."

Bishop Luke interrupted. "All well and good. What is this Jewish family requesting?"

It took three more mugs of ale to explain the situation.

"So the bottom line is the Jews will have a small presence here unless one of the Roman leaders decides to kill them?"

"Correct."

"We have no evidence they are bad Jews."

"None whatsoever."

"Then it is our Christian duty to give them shelter."

Father Timothy surprised me. "We must insist they have their Temple. We don't want them to lose the moral code they live under.

Of course, I will do my best to bring the light to their religious leaders."

I had to grin at that. "I would suggest a private room at the inn."

"Why is that?"

"So, you will be close to the ale. Both groups will need plenty."

The bishop added, "Also, it will be good that the people of both faiths see their leaders talking."

So, we were to become the secret base of the Jews and their money. Maybe those things I had read as a child about Cabals weren't so far off.

Chapter 26

Once Bishop Luke had bought into the idea that Jews be welcome in Owen-nap, he took charge. He was more modern in his thinking than I was.

Soon after their arrival, he had the Owen-nap newspaper interview them. The interview was slanted to make them seem like, well, not a second coming, but a good thing.

He and Father Timothy wrote editorials about how they decided these were good Jews, not bad Jews. I did have to laugh a little. They had gone overboard so much that the National Inquirer might not have accepted their stories. But then again, you never knew.

One thing that amazed me was how good the paper was with its line art. They had portraits of the Goldman family that were incredibly life-like. I had always thought all Jews were Semitic in their descent. The Goldmans were Aryan in appearance. Instead of being small and swarthy, Frank was tall and blonde. His wife had light brown hair, and the kids were blonde.

This would make accepting them much easier. By the time more traditional-looking Jews appeared, I hoped that the community would have accepted them.

I took Frank on a tour of our factories and farms. He was impressed to no end with the four-field rotation and the equipment we were using. He could see how we could grow more crops using less manpower. This would give us more people for other efforts.

He met all my managers on the way. When we got to Andrew Glassman, our mirror maker, he was dancing around.

"These are worth a fortune, every single one, and you can make many at a time. How can you do that?"

"It will be easier to show you than tell you."

This led to a trip to my chemistry station. I introduced him to Peter Owen-nap and had Peter give his dog and pony show of the steps needed to make silver nitrate.

Before the demonstration started, he wanted to know about Peter's eyeglasses. He had seen them in a shop in London, but never anyone wearing them. That led to questions about the material the frames were made of.

After an hour of this, he finally watched the demonstration.

Frank's first question was, "How did you figure out all these steps?"

"Trial and error with many experiments along the way."

I wasn't about to tell him about my history. I also didn't take him to the lab run by Jude Glassman. I considered that a state secret.

At the crossbow factory, he was very quiet. Again, he was given a demonstration by a three-person team. There were two women and a man. The women were the senior personnel.

As we were leaving, I asked him what he thought.

"Owen-nap is going to be a force to be reckoned with. I think enough of these teams, and you could take on any army worldwide."

I'm vain enough that I took him to the next field exercise that our not so small anymore army was carrying out. We now could field a thousand soldiers.

We had even found enough horses for sale that we had a mounted force. They would be scouts and would be a valuable addition.

I had to skirt us around a secret item we were working on.

I had the Bishop and Father Timothy in on this from the beginning. Jude Glassman had built a small hydrogen generator for me. Dissolving zinc in a hydrochloric bath gave off hydrogen gas and zinc oxide.

For the balloon, we tried paper-lined linen fabric. Our model was six feet tall and about four feet around. We had a small basket underneath to show that weights could be lifted. We used about forty pounds, including the weight of the basket.

I wanted to demonstrate that there were gases lighter than air and that they could be used to lift men in the air. The goal was to have observation balloons.

When the Bishop and the Priest saw the balloon rise into the air, they weren't pleased. Evidentially this was a bridge too far.

"If God wanted man to fly, he would have given us wings."

That statement by the bishop was kindness. After that, words like witchcraft and the devil's work were used. I shut the project down immediately. Telling the gentlemen that I wouldn't make any advances against the Church.

I also suggested that a letter be sent to the Pope asking if there were any teachings about a man being lifted into the air by a physical device.

At the same time, I was still collecting linen panels and having them lined with paper. If we desperately needed an observation balloon, I would ask forgiveness.

I even considered moving Jude Glassman to someplace further away, like Hilston, so the bishop couldn't constantly check up on the operation. Maybe it should be a standalone project under someone else.

The linen weavers I was using were in Hilston, so that is why I thought of moving the project there. The weavers were told that this was the backing for a tapestry.

The only way I could keep track of all my projects was through my notebooks. I wrote everything in secret code. I used English.

While Frank and I were on a horseback tour of my Districts, we had long conversations. I described Armorica and how that would become our new trade route. The town of Vellooasses was an entryway to both the Franks and Romans. Osismil and Venti, while smaller with less access, would be more discreet ports to ship from.

Frank was enthused by the opportunities this would give for trading. Also, it would be a good escape route from the Romans.

As we talked on our trip from Owen-nap to Bodmin, he saw our first semaphore tower being constructed. We were doing the Bodmin-Owen-nap chain first to work the bugs out before revealing it to the world by the Owen-nap-Saltash route.

He grasped the idea at once.

"Do you realize what an advantage this would give?"

"Why do you think we are building it?"

"Yes, but merchants could get word of disasters or shipments coming in early. They could bid on the cargo before anyone else knew."

"I understand. Our first use will be military. Knowing an enemy is approaching will give us time to move troops into place. That is why this road we are riding is in such good condition. It is for defense. It also allows us to keep our troops spread out. Each location has enough troops to defend until the rest of the army can get there."

"That is a great cost saving."

I could see that Frank and I didn't always speak the same language.

From Bodmin, we rode to the lead/silver mine at Mt. Brunwenely. He was impressed with the potential of the open pit mine. The compressed air pumps we were using amazed him. He asked if they were for sale. I told him not at this time.

I had deliberately held back from showing him the coins we had minted. I had brought several of each along with me. When I showed them to him, he got very quiet.

"You call these 'crows'?"

I explained the milling of the edges so shaving the coins would stand out.

He handled them reverently.

"These coins would make our lives so much easier. Imagine accepting a coin without weighing or assaying in extreme cases."

"That's the idea."

"As you undoubtedly know, bad money drives good money out. However, my community would only use these coins for transactions among ourselves."

"We hadn't planned to mint that many, and besides, the coins would get out, and then we would have many questions and invasion attempts."

"Could you mint special coins for us that wouldn't lead to you?"

"I'm not against it, but that would be between you and the Bishop. He certainly would want to be rewarded for coining them."

"I think we could come to an arrangement."

I thought about the negotiations between a Jewish Banker and a tight-fisted Bishop. I planned to be far away that day.

We rode from the pit mine to Hilston and from there to Wendon. Frank was able to see what was being done in these Districts. He complimented me on my even-handedness with them.

When we returned to Owen-nap, Frank asked for some time to think about things. I told him there was no hurry. I had some thinking of my own to do.

Before I got involved in a war with Tintagel, I had to get my own backyard in order. That meant I had to come to arrangements with Brude, Caustock, Fowey, Redruth,

Gaberton, Pensilva, Lewanniet, and
Bolventor.

Redruth and Fowey would be the easiest as I
had already met the leaders and were on
good terms. I had messages sent to the
Barons and asked them to meet me in
Saltash.

On the appointed day, both Barons were
present. We met in the Saltash Keep. The
old Baron had graciously allowed its use.
Even though he had yielded it to me, I felt
like it was his home, so I asked him each
time I wanted to stay or use it for a meeting.

After welcoming them and setting them at
ease with a mug of ale, I made my pitch.

"My Lords, nothing is secret for long around
here, so you must have heard that Tintagel
will be casting its eyes on Owen-nap."

Exchanging looks, Baron Fowey replied,
"We have. Also, if we keep 'My Lording'
and 'Baroning,' we will be here forever. I'm
Andrew, and this is Tom."

"I'm James."

"Okay, James, what are you asking for?"

That was direct and to the point. I also didn't
miss the, 'Okay.'

"I would like you to become part of my
Viscounty; you would remain as Barons,
and I would not require any tribute. I would
require that you do not provide Tintagel
with any help. Undoubtedly, you have seen

the improvements that I have made in my Districts. I would be willing to help finance you to reach our level."

Andrew turned to Tom and handed him a silver.

"You win, Tom."

Tom took the coin and explained, "We speculated what you would ask of us on the ride over. I bet that you would want us to join you."

Both men were smiling, so it seemed they were agreeable.

Tom continued, "However, we won't accept that deal."

My heart dropped.

Andrew added, "We want to swear fealty to you and become a real part of Owen-nap."

I stuttered out, "Why?"

"Because we are so close neighbors that whatever fate gives you, we will share. Besides, loyalty goes two ways. You would have to help defend us if needed. We have seen how you honor your words, so we are confident this is the best for us."

"How soon can I come to your Baronies and conduct the ceremony?"

"The sooner, the better," said Andrew. "I envy you and your road system and want one in Fowey as soon as possible."

"Could you tell me the attitude of Caustock and Brude?"

"Simple, they want to join you as soon as possible. They thought you would have invaded them a long time ago. Becoming part of your Viscounty and keeping their power is much more than expected."

"That is great!"

Tom added, "they have seen the improvements at Wendon and want them. More importantly, their people want them so much they have been voting with their feet and moving into Owen-nap. The Barons will be happy to stop losing their people."

We spent the rest of the day planning on absorbing the Baronies into Owen-nap. By dinner time, we had too many ales and weren't making much sense, so we retired for the day.

The next day, we three hung-over Barons continued our planning.

Chapter 27

At least those to the south and west of me had joined with no problems. I still had the others to worry about.

Gaberton saved me from having to contact them. They attacked Pirthtowan. That proved a big mistake as we could move supporting troops to Pirthtowan as the garrison held out.

The semaphore system wasn't installed that far yet, so we didn't get an early warning. The roads from Bodmin to Pirthtowan had been improved so that we could force march four crossbow squads plus four squads of spearmen to protect them on the battlefield in one day. By noon the next day, we would have five hundred soldiers on the field.

A squad was five crossbows firing constantly, with the support of two others. That meant we could fire one hundred and twenty-five bolts a minute for about half an hour.

Since Gaberton only had one hundred armsmen on the field, this should be more than enough. I wasn't with the first group but would arrive early the next day. When I arrived, all was over but the shouting. We had killed forty Gaberton armsmen, including their Baron when the rest surrendered.

When my main body of men arrived, we proceeded to Gaberton to take the Barony. The gates were wide open when we got there, and the Keep was deserted. The Baron's wife and children had fled with the Baron's silver to parts unknown. I wasn't inclined to chase them and face the problem of any sons becoming a symbol of resistance.

Even there, we got lucky. There were no sons, just daughters. I guess someone could marry the oldest and claim to be the Baron by right of marriage. Since the oldest girl was only five, it would be some years down the road.

No one in this time period would marry a five-year-old girl. Who knew if she could have children?

I couldn't figure out why Baron Gaberton attacked Pirthtowan. He had to know that even if he took it, he couldn't hold it and that we could take his Keep easily. It made no sense.

With Thad taking notes, I went about the job of incorporating Gaberton as one of our Districts. The village Headman could give me no clue as to why the Baron had acted as he did. The only clue he had was that the Baron's wife and daughters were fleeing to Tintagel. It seems her father was high in King Geraint's councils.

Maybe someday I could ask Geraint if he knew.

Leaving a force of fifty soldiers to hold the Keep, I marched my remaining four hundred and fifty to Pensilva. Since we had come this far, we might as well settle the issues now.

It took us two days to reach Pensilva. Eleanor remained behind and worked with John Steward to provide a logistics train with food and plenty of crossbow bolts.

When we arrived at Pensilva, a rider with a white flag exited the Keep. He had a message from Baron Pensilva asking to parley.

I agreed, and a tent was set up in the field before the Keep. We agreed that the Baron and I would only be accompanied by two armsmen.

I cheated and had crossbowmen stationed one hundred feet from the tent. They could easily take out his guards. Hey, I'm not stupid. These were the dark ages, noted for treachery.

Thankfully none of that was needed. Baron Pensilva wanted to assure me he had nothing to do with Gaberton's plans.

I asked him if he knew what they were.

"He didn't want to yield to you, so he communicated with King Geraint. The plan was for him to take Pirthtowan but not try to keep it. He and his men would return to Gaberton, where his wife and daughters awaited, take all the silver, and retreat to Tintagel.

"King Geraint talked him into it to find out your strengths. He promised Gaberton a position in his court as a reward.

"He asked me, Baron Lewanniet, and Baron Bolventor to join him. We all told him he was crazy. When he didn't breach Pirthtowan walls the first day, he should have run."

I asked him a few more questions. I had only met him briefly once before. I liked his forthright way of talking. He was in his early twenties and was good-looking, at least my guards had assured me as he approached. They were both women, so they knew better than I.

I asked him about his family.

"I'm single, My Lord. My parents died from the grippe the last time it passed through the area. I was forced to take over and have not had time to court any women."

From the murmurs behind me, I think there were two volunteers.

I asked Baron Pensilva, "where would you like to go from here?"

"I think you are in a position to dictate that."

"True. Would you like to retain your Barony and have me as your liege Lord?"

"Would we have the benefits that all your other Barons have?"

"Certainly."

"Then I accept. Frankly, I'm over my head with this Baron business. If you could provide me with a Steward who knows what he is going to do, it would be a blessing."

"What about your current Head Steward?"

"He died the same time as my parents. I have tried my best, but I know it is not good enough. I suspect some of my guardsmen are about to overthrow me."

There was a coughing sound behind him. He turned and looked at the guard.

The guard spoke up, "Most of us support you, My Lord, and you haven't been doing that bad of a job."

I noticed the other guard start to draw his sword.

I shouted, "Ware swordsman."

A crossbow bolt slammed into the guard's chest before his sword was completely out of its scabbard.

The young Baron was staring at me wide-eyed.

"We would never have had a chance, would we?"

"No, you wouldn't have, I'm not much older than you, but I'm old in the ways of war."

The remaining guard added, "see, I told you that you were not doing bad, My Lord."

This statement relaxed the tension, and we all laughed. Once we settled down, I explained to the young Baron how we integrated new territory into our Viscounty.

"First, the surveyors will start. They will look at your existing road system and see if it can be improved. Once a plan is developed, with your approval, of course, our road building teams will start improving the system.

"At the same time, a census will be held so we know how many people there are and what their capabilities are. Simultaneously modern farming methods will be introduced. This will be the hardest part as farmers as a lot are hidebound traditionalists who feel that if it worked for Granddad, why change it."

He laughed at that.

"I have already learned that lesson. I tried to introduce your new plows, and there was so much resistance I gave up."

"We will send some of your more open-minded farmers to Owen-nap to see how successful we have been. Some of our people will come back with them to provide on site instruction on what to do.

"We will also review all your food storage and waste removal systems. I will turn our

Lady Agnes loose on your village to clean it up and introduce modern sanitation.

"Once those basic items are under control, we will get the real work started."

The Baron asked, "I'm half afraid to ask, what is the real work?"

"Starting schools, opening an orphanage, seeing what products or materials your Baronage can produce to provide a steady income for you and your people.

"Oh yeah, bring your troops up to our standards and fortify your Keep better than it is now. The list is long."

You could see I had overloaded the young Baron's mind, so I asked if we could assemble his citizens the next morning. He would swear an oath to me and become part of the Middle Counties.

"Yes, let's get started."

I liked his attitude. I would speak to Eleanor about finding him a wife. It would be good for him to have a helpmate.

The next day we held the oath-taking ceremony. Everyone within walking distance attended. He was cheered after swearing his allegiance to me, a good sign.

One of Eleanor's supply trains had caught up with us, and included food for a feast, so we had a feast to celebrate the occasion. Free food and drink always went down well.

While not a fair, we had people in our train who could juggle and do acrobatics. Four of our men had a quartet which was rather good. In my day and age, we called them Barber Shop Quartets. It all made for a good time.

The next day we journeyed on to Lewanniet. It took a day and a half to get there. Every night we camped on the road, I had fortifications and many guards on duty. Safe drinking water was identified, and latrine pits were dug away from them. While not up to the old Roman standards, we were safe.

It occurred to me that since things were going to get serious in the near future, I should probably be building a fort every night. We could carry the wall sections in wagons along with the tools to dig the pit in front of the walls. The dirt would be thrown on our side of the pit. The new wall created from the dirt would be the base for our walls.

Like the Romans, we would have four gates so we could issue out in any direction. We would have to send scouts further out every day to select camping sites large enough.

We already had a group of moveable kitchens similar in concept to the Old West chuck wagons.

We had no trouble getting to Lewanniet. Once there, I sent a rider out with a white flag as they hadn't opened their gates or sent their own messenger out.

Baron Pensilva was with me. He made a point of riding almost out to where our flag man was waiting and waved to some people on the wall.

He must have been recognized and not seen to be under duress because the gates were opened soon after. A small party rode out to greet us.

The leader was obviously Baron Lewanniet. He was accompanied by two guards and a handsome young lady about Pensilvas age.

"Baron Lewanniet, I have come to talk about the recent attack on Pirthtowan by the late Baron Gaberton.

I had also met Baron Lewanniet once before. I remembered his name was Thomas. Today he was wearing a red robe, which was his color.

I noticed the young lady was also in red, so I assumed she was Thomas's daughter. Pensilva was in his blue. While an open tent was being set up to provide shade, tables and chairs were brought up, and we introduced ourselves.

I was correct that Joan Lewanniet was the Baron's daughter and heir. She had no brothers that lived beyond birth, Thomas explained. His wife could bear no more children, so she was it. He informed me that she had been in training to run the Barony since she was a small child.

He told me that she was always serious in her demeanor and outlook on life. This statement was punctuated by a girlish giggle. He turned in surprise at his daughter.

She didn't notice him as she was engrossed with Baron Pensilva. He didn't notice us either as he was returning her gaze.

Thomas and I looked at each other and shrugged.

I said, "Young love."

Thomas had a thoughtful look and said, "that could work."

I took a chance and told him, "If you join my Viscounty of the Middle Counties with me as your liege, I will guarantee her inheritance."

He didn't hesitate at all.

"I accept. The same terms as Pensilva?"

Chapter 28

After that, there were hours of discussion, but it was done. The two children contributed to the conversation when they weren't making eyes at each other.

I don't think I would need Eleanor to find him a wife. They had found each other.

I asked, "Thomas, how do you think Baron Bolventor will react?"

"I'm not sure. Robert is a stubborn man and is used to getting his way. At the same time, he wants the best for his people. He has been a good Baron. I know he worries about the looming war between you and King Geraint."

"How did you hear about that?"

"Everyone in Cornwall knows of it. Your people haven't talked about it, but Geraint's people have boasted how they are going to take your silver mine.

"That and his spies have been asking questions about your Barony, or Viscounty as you call it. By the way, why do you call it a country? I have never heard of that title."

"In some areas of the world, there is a progress of titles. It starts with Baron, goes to Count, then Earl, Duke, King, and Emperor. A Viscount is a Baron on the verge of gaining control of many Baronies to become a Count."

"That implies that you intend to take over more Baronies."

I had to laugh at that,

"What do you think happened the last two days?"

He got a chagrined look.

"I didn't think of it that way. I just saw Lewanniet joining a larger force."

"And so you have, but we have to call the leader something different than Baron. I choose Viscount for now. Now, back to Bolventor, do you have any recommendations on how to approach him."

"Let me explain what has happened. He is aware of the improvements you have made and will want them for his people. At the same time, he won't want to be on the losing end of a war."

"How many troops can King Geraint field?"

"He fielded two thousand against King Ine and lost, so I expect it is half that now."

"I can field over one thousand right now, not counting soldiers for Brude, Caustock, Fowey, Redruth, Gaberton, your Lewanniet, and Pensilva. These have all joined the Middle Counties in the last two weeks. Even at twenty men per Barony, it is an additional one hundred and seventy-five soldiers. Plus, our weapons are better.

"We will outnumber him, and I have scouts out looking for the most favorable battlefield for us."

The Baron looked confused. "How can you choose a battlefield? I always thought armies marched until they came together."

"We have already determined that only two practical routes exist for him. Now, we have to pick the place to intercept him. Ideally, he would have to cross a river to get to us on top of a hill."

I didn't mention that I would love to have them in a flood plain when they crossed the river or even another hill at a right angle to the first so we could have an enfilade or flanking fire.

"If you are still willing, I want you to start Bolventor tomorrow. It will take you two days to get there. My armsmen and I will start the next day, which will take three days. That gives you two days to talk to the Baron.

"Please clarify to him that he either swears allegiance or gets conquered. I've run out of time. Winter is about done, and King Geraint will be marching from Tintagel in the early spring."

Baron Lewanniet stated, "I would think he would wait until the spring planting was done."

"Normally, yes, but he will want to surprise me as much as possible."

"What about your spring planting?"

"We have enough farmers with modern equipment to plant and still field our army. Feel free to share all of this with Baron Bolventor."

'I will."

"King Geraint has only two choices of routes, and both of them converge on Bolventor. I would think the Baron would want our army on the far side from here to meet him."

"Agreed."

Early the next day, Baron Lewanniet and his daughter headed to Bolventor. I wouldn't want to leave my daughter where she could get up to mischief with Baron Pensilva, either.

The day after that, my troops and I started our march to Bolventor. Since winter was almost over, we had to walk through cold rain most of the way. It put me in a sour mood. I almost hoped that Baron Bolventor resisted.

He didn't.

As we approached his Keep, the gates were opened, and the two Barons, Lewanniet and Bolventor, were waiting for us. My troops were taken to a barracks to warm up and dry out. Their stablemen took care of our horses.

Baron Pensilva was with me. He claimed he wanted to see how the negotiations went but only wanted to negotiate with one person. She seemed to be open to his offers.

I'm certain I would never have these worries with my Catherine. Dream on.

It is surprising what a mulled ale and a fire will do to your mood. What they called a mulled ale was fortified with a spirit without any other fixings. It was still good.

The green-clad Baron Bolventor was a genial host. I don't see how Baron Lewanniet saw him as being stubborn.

"Owen-nap, I understand you want me to swear allegiance to you and your Viscounty?"

"That is correct."

"Thomas has explained the facts of life to me. I don't believe in fighting losing battles, so I will take an oath to you."

"I'm glad to hear that, My Lord."

A little sugar helps the medicine go down, according to Mary Poppins. You could tell even that little courtesy made things easier for him.

"So how do we go about this?" he asked.

"Have your guards inform the people that they are needed in the courtyard, especially the village Headman. Do you have a priest?"

"He died last year, and the Archbishop in Tintagel has yet to appoint a new one."

"That has been the same in every Barony I have joined with. I wonder why he won't appoint anyone?'

"That's easy. No one has the money to buy the appointment. Usually, it is the youngest son of a Baron, but there seems to be a shortage of them around here."

"Collect the people, and I will take your oath in the courtyard. That way, all will see that it is given freely."

"Hmmph."

"I know, but you are doing this of your own free will?"

He sighed. "Yes, My Lord, I would rather be independent, but that isn't going to happen. It is you or King Geraint."

"Things will be better under me than him."

"That is why I have chosen to do this."

The people were gathered in two hours, about twenty of them including the Headman and his wife. There were enough witnesses that the word would get out that Baron Bolventor did this freely.

When he decided to do something, he did it right. He made a brief speech to his people that our methods and improvements would benefit the people greatly, as opposed to the heavier and heavier taxes King Geraint had been imposing. My taxes were only a quarter of what Geraint had been taking. People cheered at that.

When we were done, the Baron asked what my next steps would be. He, Lewanniet, and I sat down with Thad, and I had Thad read off his checklist of items to be done.

Baron Bolventor was impressed. The list was of things we would be doing for him and nothing he had to give us other than cooperation in making it happen.

While we were meeting, Baron Pensilva and Lewanniet's daughter were mysteriously missing. I wonder what they were up to? I don't know if it was love, lust, or infatuation, but those two had it bad.

When we were finished, Lewanniet went off to find his wayward daughter while Bolventor and I continued our talks.

"Baron, there are two routes that King Geraint can take to get to my open pit mine. They both come together here. Do you know of any good defensive spots after the two routes converge?"

"There is one spot that would be perfect if you are looking for what I think you are."

"Is it far?"

"A half-day's ride.

"Could we possibly ride out there tomorrow and take a look?"

"Certainly, it is in my best interest for you to win."

At least he got that.

The next day, we made the trip to the spot the Baron thought would work. All my people accompanied me as they did not need to garrison Bolventor's Keep. He was committed at this point.

Baron Lewanniet came along to see what the position looked like. He made his daughter accompany him, and Pensilva trailed along like a puppy dog. I don't think he even knew where we were going or cared. He would follow Joan to the ends of the earth.

I understood that feeling.

When we arrived at the site, I had to agree with Baron Bolventor. The path was between two hills. It would narrow Geraint's forces to about six men wide.

As the path emerged from the hills, it turned sharply to the left, where another hill kept them from going straight.

The hills could be climbed from the path, but it would not be easy. The path between the hills was over two miles long, so we could let his entire army pass before we blocked his retreat. Once they passed the entrance to the pass through the hills, we would block it off by assembling a barrier across the road. It would be built-in sections that could be put together quickly. It would even have firing steps for the crossbow troops.

The hills on both sides of the path would be lined with crossbow troops. The spearmen would protect them from any of Geraint's people who made it to the top.

King Geraint's scouts would be allowed to turn to the left. When they were far enough down the road not to be heard, they would be taken out. Then, the road would be blocked with more of the portable palisades.

We would have them in a kill box. What could go wrong?

I hit myself up the side of the head for even thinking that. Baron Lewanniet gave me an odd look but said nothing.

I gathered the Barons and my Sergeants and explained my plans. I asked for any thoughts they may have.

One of my Senior Sergeants said, "Shouldn't we look at the other end of the pass before we jump to conclusions?"

"That is why you are a Senior Sergeant, Sergeant Farmer."

We rode the trail to where it entered the hills. What we saw almost kiboshed the plan.

Before the hills closed in, there was a wide open plain. Where would we hide our troops until Geraint's army passed?

Again my Sergeants came through.

"We could build a barrow and hide behind that."

That made sense as barrows dotted the land. The ancient burial sites seemed to have no rhyme or reason for their placement. Maybe it was where a leader died in battle?

It sounded so good that there had to be something wrong with the idea.

Senior Sergeant Farmer pointed out that if any of King Geraint's scouts had been on this route before, they would wonder where it had come from and ride over to examine it.

I hate it when a plan doesn't come together.

Chapter 29

And I love it when a plan comes together.

"I know what we will do," I told the group.

"Thad, please hand me a wax tablet."

He gave me one of the several tablets he carried for such an occasion.

"Instead of building a hill, we will make the land slope up gently."

As I said this, I sketched out an upslope on flat ground.

"The slope will be such that the ground will rise five feet in one hundred feet. That is slight enough that no one would think much of it.

"We will get the dirt needed from a reversed sloped trench which will be the same height and length."

On the wax tablet, I drew a flat line to represent the current ground. Then I drew a right-angle triangle with its highest point away from the road.

I drew another right-angle triangle with the long side parallel to the ground and the short side against the end of the other triangle.

The hypotenuse of the right triangle would be the upslope. The result would be a pit hidden by the gentle upslope.

"We will cut the sod from the top of the pit and use it to cover the newly created slope."

Everyone was nodding as they understood what I wanted.

"Let's check the soil over here. We're out of luck if there are stones six inches down."

We were in luck. Test holes dug went down five feet. That meant we would have a ten-foot depression to hide the wall sections.

I had the area to be used staked out. We didn't have enough picks or shovels to do the job today. Leaving most of the men camped out. We went back to Lewanniet.

The next morning, we returned to the ambush site with a wagonload of picks and shovels. We also brought large squares of cloth to place the freshly dug sod on and plenty of water to keep it fresh.

There would also be wagon loads of stone brought in because it might rain and leave our freshly dug pit a muddy mess.

Excess dirt would be spread out away from the area. The wall sections could be handled by four men. We spread small gravel from the pit to the road. It wasn't so thick that it would show through the grass but would give firm footing for the men.

It took two days to prepare the ambush site. While the digging was going on, there was a small team building the wall sections.

Once these were completed and the pit and access road were in place, we had several rehearsals. The men were able to put up the wall sections within half an hour. This was quick enough for our needs, and the men now had experience at doing it.

Now all we had to do was wait. It would be no more than three weeks before the King would arrive. Since I had no idea when that would be, I had scouts near Tintagel to give us word when the King's army was on its way.

Messengers were sent to all of my Districts, requiring them to send their forces. They were to keep enough troops to defend their Keeps.

The bulk of my forces from Owen-nap were on their way along with a logistics train with enough food to last two months. They also had thousands upon thousands of crossbow bolts and spare crossbows.

Lady Agnes sent a staffed field hospital. She still couldn't understand why I called them MASH units.

I stayed at Lewanniet's Keep. Baron Bolventor also stayed with his daughter. He wanted to see how things turned out. Since Joan was there, Pensilva also stayed. I figured they would get married soon, as I suspected she was pregnant.

Barons Lewanniet, Bolventor, and I were having ale in Baron Lewanniet's office.

Baron Bolventor started with, "Viscount Owen-nap, I have never seen such a detailed battle plan put together so quickly."

Lewanniet added, "your plan could be scaled up for a much larger army, even thousands of men. Where did you learn to do that?"

I couldn't say, West Point Military Academy and the battlefields of Europe and Asia in fifty years with armies of millions of men.

Somehow, I didn't think they would believe me.

"I read a treatise on logistics some years ago, and it made sense. Make a plan and bring your men and the materials together, and you will do well."

"What is the name of this treatise?"

"The Art of War."

"Who wrote it?"

"Some man named Sun Tzu; the name is very foreign, so I don't know where it came from."

Both Barons indicated they would like to find a copy as mine had been lost. Who knew if they might find one? It was written about 500 BC. If nothing else, I could dictate a copy for my men. I have read it several times for past studies.

The next day a scout rode in from the forward pass.

"Viscount Owen-nap, a rider has come from Tintagel asking for you."

"Is he being allowed through?"

"Guards are bringing him now."

Several hours later, the guards brought to me a bland-looking man. He identified himself as King Geraint's spymaster.

I asked him why he sought me out.

"Because my spies have found out your forces and capabilities. Geraint has no way of defeating you."

"So."

"So, I have no desire to be on the losing side."

"What do you have to offer?"

"The date he plans to march, how many men and their weapons, his route, and his supply train."

"Do you know what he plans to do once he takes the pit mine?"

"Yes."

"What are you asking for this information?"

"Five thousand silver and safe conduct to a port in Armorica."

"Why aren't you asking to join me."

"From everything my spies have told me, you are no fool. If I turned my coat, you could never trust me not to do it again."

"That is true. There is one more thing I want from you. I will pay another five thousand silver for it."

"What is that?"

"The names of all your spies in my Viscounty."

"I was told you are using a funny new title. May I ask why?"

"It is hard to explain, but in time will become apparent to all."

"I will settle for that."

"Good because that is all you get. What should I call you besides spymaster?"

"Pick a good Christian name for me and use it."

"All right, Judas."

I was surprised when he broke out into laughter.

"Oh, that is funny, very funny, but true. I'm not certain how good of a name it is, but it is apt."

He continued, "I accept your offer, all the information, and the spy network for ten thousand silver."

"A deal."

The Barons and I spent the rest of the day quizzing him. We wanted to know about the troops' color of their surcoats.

While everyone asked many questions, I asked mine in different ways several times.

He finally looked at me and said, "You have played this game before."

I chuckled. The other Barons looked at me askance.

Lewanniet asked Judas what he meant.

"If you have been paying attention, Viscount Owen-nap has repeatedly asked the same question differently. He is checking to see if I'm consistent in my answers."

Both Barons looked at me.

"You seem to have many strings to your bow, My Lord. Did you read another treatise?"

"No, I was trained in this."

"Who trained you?"

"Someone from far away. They are gone now."

Better to say Counterintelligence was gone rather than not here yet.

King Geraint wasn't bringing that many troops. Only twelve hundred men. It seems his treasury was empty, and that was all he could afford.

Of the twelve hundred, only five hundred were trained soldiers. The rest were conscripted farmers. His supply train would have two weeks of food in it. After that, they would be living off the land. That meant they would be raiding farms on the way.

At first, I felt a little sorry for Geraint and his troops for what we were about to do to them, but with their plan, there would be no mercy.

Once he had the pit mine under his control, he planned on marching to Owen-nap and conquering it. All the others he thought would surrender to him.

"Judas, even if he reached the pit mine, how did he think he could take Owen-nap? You must know about our Keep and its defenses."

"I do. He thinks he can take Owen-nap's because I may not have been completely forthcoming with your strengths."

"Why?"

"There was no doubt that you could defeat him, but I didn't want you to end up weak and unable to pay me."

Despicable as he was, I had to admire his pragmatic nature.

He gave us the names of the spies, and Thad wrote them down. None of them were in positions of great trust. It seemed they, and he got much of their information from our newspapers.

Just the promotion announcements of our soldiers would tell them a lot. I had one more question for him.

"Why Armorica and not London?"

"Because London will fall to Wessex soon, and I used to work for Wessex until Tintagel bought me."

I had to shake my head at that. This guy liked to live on the edge.

"I suggest you don't stop at Armorica but continue to Rome or further."

"I may even go as far as Constantinople."

"Probably wise."

"So if you give me my silver with your leave, I will be on my way."

It was my turn to burst out laughing.

"You will get the silver when we have confirmed the troop count and arrested the spies."

"It was worth a try. Though I'm not concerned about the accuracy of the information I gave you."

Two events occurred a week later. Scouts reported that King Geraint and his men were on the move. This was the date that Judas gave us, so he had hopes of living. I would have been serious about hanging him if he lied to us.

The second event was the arrival of my troops. They had met at Looe and proceeded to Bolventor, being led by my wife.

At least she had left the baby at home. She had even arranged for Catherine to be raised by a local family who would take her to Armorica. They would be given access to a small fortune. Her bodyguard would accompany her all her life.

I had no reason to fear this, but it was good that my wife was thinking. I didn't even give her a hard time about coming along. She had proved at Looe that she could handle tough situations.

I must confess, it was good to have her at my side in bed.

Since it would take King Geraint a full three weeks to reach Bolventor, we had time to double-check all our preparations.

Eleanor had all the latest news from home. It seems Frank Goldman had decided to take my offer to be a refuge, if needed, to the families in Rome. He left his wife and children in Owen-nap. They had started school, and he didn't want to interrupt their school year.

Some things were the same no matter what day and age you lived in. Eleanor had sent guards with him as far as Armorica, and then he was alone. I hoped he was able to make the long journey safely.

If this worked out, we would end up as the banking center of the world. Take that, Switzerland.

Chapter 30

Our scouts kept track of King Geraint and his army as they left Tintagel and made their way toward Bolventor. It took them twenty-seven days to make the trip. It should have taken twenty-one days. A single horse and rider could have done it in five.

This said a lot about their organization. The scouts reported it was like three separate armies marching. Geraint and a few accompanying nobles were first in line daily to avoid the dust.

His two hundred professional soldiers followed Geraint. These two groups were organized and outmarched the main body by hours daily. Their camps would be set up hours before the rest of the camp straggling in.

The main body of eight hundred conscripted soldiers was spread out, and some groups wouldn't meet the main camp until dark. This led to chaos as the last arrived tried to put up tents without having anyone to guide them to prepared spots. There were no prepared spots.

The supply train with camp followers attached never made it to the nightly camp. Each day, they made camp a little further behind the main body. Making it harder to bring food to the camp each day.

Each night, the conscripts deserted and headed home. They had lost two hundred men when they reached our ambush. Geraint didn't know this because he sent no one back to check.

No wonder he lost to King Ine.

While they were doing their forlorn march, I had my people working on the ambush site. On the backside of each hill, there were steps dug in to provide easy access to the top.

At the base of the backsides were the troop's tents set up in orderly rows behind palisades. Latrines were dug, bathhouses set up, and cooking facilities and MASH units lined both sides of the road.

If the troops thought they were on vacation, they were mistaken. Every unit had to do warm-up exercises and a ten-mile run. After that, they had breakfast. Then, they went to a crossbow or spear practice.

All gear was inspected weekly, and anything broken or loose was replaced or repaired. Boxes of crossbow bolts were stationed below the peak of each hill.

Every night, the troops set up entertainment around their firepits. Normally, fires wouldn't be allowed, but our scouts reported that King Geraint hadn't sent any of his scouts.

The guy is an idiot.

Eleanor and I made the rounds of the different fighting units to see how they were doing. They all were in good humor. Our scout reports were shared amongst the troops, so everyone knew what was coming at us.

They all agreed the guy was an idiot.

The bishop's newspaper had a correspondent in the camp to interview people. He would send his stories back by messenger. The newspaper was weekly, but three extra editions were put on for this event.

When I was interviewed, I told them we were confident and that I had the best army to be fielded.

I had made a request to Father Timothy, and he came through. He came into the camp's headquarters area late in the evening two days later. He was riding the most decrepit mule I had ever seen.

The mule looked like he would keel over any minute. Father Timothy didn't look much better. I suspect this was the longest trip he had ever done.

He was accompanied by two altar boys leading the second-worst mules I had ever seen. I tried to figure out which one was the saddest looking and decided the two mules were tied.

The altar boys, who looked about ten years old, were all smiles, looking around. To them, this was a great adventure.

My Senior Sergeant took charge of the heavily laden mules and the two altar boys. One mule carried their camping gear, the other accouterments for a mass. Father Timothy had even brought the large wooden cross from the front of the Church.

I helped Father Timothy down from his mule, escorted him into my main tent and arranged for a late meal.

When the meal arrived, Father Timothy was sound asleep, sitting upright in a chair. Two of my men carried him to a spare tent for the night.

The next morning, Father Timothy appeared in the dining tent in much better shape. At least he looked like he had some sleep. He was still walking like he was stiff and sore all over.

"Father Timothy, it must have been a hard trip for you,"

"It was. The demon spawn of a mule that ran off twice, and we spent an extra day chasing him down."

"I would have let him go. You could have walked faster than he was moving yesterday."

"I borrowed him from the Monastery."

"I think they took advantage of you when they gave that mule to you."

"I know they did. The payback will be heavenly."

"I've never heard it put that way before."

"The payback will be heavenly. For me."

With perfect timing, Eleanor came into the dining tent.

She said, "I've bad news. Father Timothy's mule died last night."

She looked at us strangely when we both burst out laughing. We had to explain why it was so funny. She didn't get it.

When we settled down, I told the good Father, "Don't worry, I will find you a better mount."

"Don't hurry. It will take me a couple of days to heal from that mule ride."

That set us off again. Once more, Eleanor didn't get it. Maybe females don't have a sense of humor. But I knew that wasn't true because she laughed at me many times.

"Father, when do you want to do the mass for all the troops?"

"When do you think King Geraint will arrive?"

"He is two days out at last report."

"Let's hold the mass tonight in case he arrives early."

I knew there was no chance of that, but I agreed to have it that evening.

The Father spent the afternoon hearing confessions. There must have been a short confession as he ran them through quickly. That or this group of soldiers never sinned. Ha!

That night the troops were all assembled on the training grounds well away from the hills which had the pass.

It was an impressive sight to see an army of over one thousand troops having mass. The ceremony was carried out by torchlight under a clear starlit night. This was more impressive than any Church I had ever been to.

During the wars in my time, you would never have gathered this many men together near a battlefield. Between bombing, strafing, and mortar fire, it would have been a disaster.

I don't know how he did it, but Father Timothy's voice carried loud and clear to the troops.

It took almost two hours for communion that evening, so many soldiers had received absolution. It was strange what the possibility of death on the battlefield would do to a man's mind.

All in all, it was a moving experience. The men marched quietly off the field when the priest told us to go in peace. The quiet lasted the rest of the evening as the men sat about their campfires.

As clear and bright as the last several days had been, the morning was overcast, with storm clouds moving in from the north.

Scouts reported that rain had already started on King Geraint's columns, and the road they were on was turning into a muddy quagmire. They had made less than five miles and came to a stop.

It would be at least two more days before they arrived. It was always hurry up and wait in war. When the wait was over, events would be like a freight train.

You would be standing there fat, dumb, and happy one minute, then fighting for your life the next.

It took two days for the storm front to move through. My army stayed as dry as possible in their tents. Geraint's army kept miserably marching on, making only a few miles.

I was all for this. My men would be fed, warm, and well-rested. Geraint's would be hungry, cold, and tired.

Eleanor, Lewanniet, Bolventor, and Father Timothy were sipping hot coffee when I opened a conversation.

"Father Timothy, the mass you gave was wonderful. Can I gift you something for doing this?"

I had in mind a new altar cloth or something of that nature.

The good Father sat up and replied, "Some of the villages in the districts are large enough to support a Church. You could build them for them."

Now I was between a rock and a hard place. I had made the offer, and he had accepted.

Not to appear stingy in front of the Barons, I replied, "It will be done. Let me know what villages are large enough, and I will make it happen."

"Thank you, Viscount Owen-nap. I knew your generosity knew no bounds, so I have a list."

He then handed the list over to the ever-present Thad, who handled such things for me.

Before I could say anything else, Father Timothy continued.

"There is one other thing. I imagine that the Archbishop of Tintagel will be replaced by Bishop Luke. If so, could I buy the Bishopric for Owen-nap?"

"I hadn't thought about it, but you are correct. Bishop Luke would become Archbishop Luke of Cornwall. If so, you are welcome to take his place as Bishop Owen-nap."

"Thank you, My Lord. There is one small issue that I would need your help with."

"What is that?"

"Bishop Luke had to pay five thousand silver to buy his Bishopric. He expects the same from me. Could I impose upon you for a loan:"

"How would you repay me?"

"From the seigniorage earned by minting coins."

"Of course."

I would mine and refine the silver. The bishop would allow us to mint coins. I would be paying for everything.

I wanted to say no but chickened out in front of the Barons.

"I will have the coins sent to the bishop."

"There is no need for that. He has agreed to have the money transferred from your account to his at the Bank of Owen-nap."

I wondered if Father Timothy would go to confession after sandbagging me like this. He and that fat Bishop Luke were turning into a pair of thieves.

I think Father Timothy knew he had pushed his luck as far as it could go as he quickly took his leave of us.

Once he was gone, Eleanor burst out laughing.

"James, I have never seen you outdone like that before."

"He blindsided me," I grumbled.

Baron Bolventor said, "and a fine blindside it was. He knew you wouldn't say no in front of us."

I darkly replied, "the payback will be heavenly, to quote Father Timothy."

"Heavenly, I thought paybacks were hell."

"Hell for him, heavenly for me."

The rain had stopped overnight, and by noon, the roads and hillsides were dried out. I, Eleanor, and my Senior Sergeant, accompanied by Barons Bolventor, Lewanniet, Pensilva, and Lewanniet's daughter, walked the top of the hills overlooking the pass.

It was the first time we had seen Pensilva and Joan in three days. Again, I wonder what they had been up to.

Everything was ready to go. The barricade teams at both ends of the pass demonstrated they could move the wooden sections in place quickly. I estimated a half hour for all. Since Geraint's army was so slow, this was more than good enough.

Along the top of the pass, the troops had made a road along the military crest. This was on the reverse slope and was just below the actual hill crest. They could move troops without being seen from down low. There were firing steps placed every few feet. We would safely fire down on the enemy without being exposed to their fire.

Our preparations were as complete as we could get them. Now, all we could do was wait. I had no doubt about our victory, it was the waiting that made me nervous.

The wait wasn't long. Two days later, the scouts reported that King Geraint and his men were camping just before the entrance to the pass.

They were on the far side of the road by our hidden wall sections. If they found them, all the planning would have been for naught.

It was a nervous night, but King Geraint and his men didn't show any curiosity about the area. They made camp, lit fires, ate, and went to sleep.

The scouts reported that even the leadership was exhausted. The next morning, they rose late and got underway.

They say plans do not survive contact with the enemy' and our plan wasn't surviving.

It wasn't any cleverness on Geraint's part or failure to work the plan on ours. I should have seen it a few days ago. His army was so spread out that we couldn't catch all of them in our ambush.

King Geraint, his nobles, and professional soldiers would have gone into the mountain pass and been stopped at the barricade. And the main body of troops wouldn't have even entered the narrow pass.

We had a hurried war council with the Senior Sergeants and my entourage, including the Barons. Even Lewanniet's daughter and Baron Pensilva were present and, for once, listening in rather than pawing all over each other.

Our options were limited. We could either pull back and meet them on a plain battlefield or refuse the pass to them.

We decided to refuse the pass. We would put the wall sections in place after Geraint and his professionals entered the pass.

The enemy would reach the second barricade and stop. Then they would be too far from the first barricade to return before it was moved into place.

When the leadership group was stopped at the second barricade, fire arrows would be shot down the line to indicate it was time to move the first wall sections into place.

I hoped we could defeat the first group in the pass before the second arrived. If so, we would send another set of arrows ordering the wall sections to be hidden again. Once the main body passed the mountain pass opening, the walls would be moved back into position. Resetting the trap.

It wasn't very easy and depended on timing. If we timed it right, there would be less danger for my troops. Paraphrasing Patton, "Let the other guy die for his country."

If the timing was wrong, we would still win, but would lose a lot of men if Geraint's soldiers made it up the sides of the pass.

A hurried plan but the best we could do. Even though I was still a little angry at Father Timothy, I wished he was here to give blessings and last rites if needed.

Since we didn't know how many days it would be before the battle, the good Father and his altar boys had returned to Owen-nap. No matter how mad, I couldn't make him ride a mule back. Besides, none of our mules were as sad as his.

Instead, they were all mounted on five horses. One each for the men and two to carry the gear. Eleanor and I waved them off, then turned back to our war plans.

King Geraint finally entered the pass three days later. Scouts had been giving us an almost hourly update on their progress. It was incredible to believe, but Geraint never put any scouts of his own out to see if we were aware of his coming.

I was still concerned about the main body being behind. It could upset our ambush.

It turned out I was worried for nothing. King Geraint and his two hundred professionals entered the pass. The main body camped three miles before the pass entrance.

That meant that we could stop Geraint at the second barrier, defeat his forces, and then let the main body through, rinse, and repeat. Except there would be no army left to repeat.

It went down exactly like that. The King and his men came to the second barrier. They barely had time to stop when I ordered my men to open fire on the King and his entourage.

None of the silly stuff like honorable combat. In my world winner takes all. I grew up in the Ardennes Forest, the Chosin Reservoir, and the jungles of Asia.

Fifty crossbow fighters sent bolts into him and his fourteen hangers-on. I had identified the former Hilston Steward's son among them and Archbishop of Tintagel from his clothing.

As ordered, the crossbow fighters fired one bolt each, decapitating the army's leadership.

After that, we waited to see what the professional soldiers' reaction would be. They sat in silence for what seemed like forever, but it was only a minute. Two Sergeants huddled together and made a decision. One of them pulled out a white cloth and tied it to his lance and rode forward.

My Senior Sergeant at the wooden wall section had one section moved aside and went out to meet them. They talked for a while, then I was signaled to come forward.

Accompanied by ten guards, I came out. Ten guards couldn't stop treachery, but they showed we had force.

Our conversation was brief. If they surrendered, they would be allowed to return to Tintagel. They only had to drop their weapons. I knew they were professionals when they didn't drop their weapons. They laid them carefully on the ground.

After that, we opened the barricade and had them march to the other side. They sat in a field around the corner from the pass. Where a field kitchen was set up to feed them. They were also given picks and shovels to dig their latrines.

They were informed they would camp here until we had the main body of conscripts under control. It might take several days.

I had an opportunity to ask one of the Sergeants if he knew why they didn't send scouts out.

"King Geraint didn't think it was worth it. He knew you would and didn't care since his army would overrun yours with ease."

"You know how that worked out."

"He was so egotistical he thought he was the smartest strategist around."

"He learned the hard way."

"It doesn't get any harder."

It took two more days before the conscript force broke camp and marched into the pass. Once they were out of sight of the first barricade, they were moved into place.

We now had them bottled up in the pass. When their lead unit, if it could be called a unit, reached the second barricade, it came to a halt.

My Senior Sergeant waved a white flag from the top of the barricade. After they produced their own, a section was opened for me and my guards to approach them. I think our defensives had them cowed, or maybe it was King Geraint's body suspended from the palisade.

Our terms were simple, drop your weapons, and go home. We would give them two weeks of provisions to see them on their way.

They would march in blocks of fifty. A smaller band might be tempted to get into mischief. Each block of fifty would have a block of fifty of my troops between them. Altogether there would be two thousand men marching to Tintagel.

They agreed to the terms. When they started to split into blocks of fifty, a problem came to light. Some of the men had no homes to return to. They had been conscripted off the streets of Tintagel or one of its Baronies.

After discussing it with my war advisors, I had word sent out that anyone who had no home needed to meet by the second barricade.

There were ninety-four men waiting. They could join the Tintagel soldiers or my army if they were physically fit. If not fit, they could proceed to Owen-nap, where they would be found employment.

The homeless were run through a MASH unit and given physicals. Eighty-seven proved fit and were given a choice of either army. They split about even with forty-one to mine and forty-seven to Tintagel. The others were to go to Owen-nap with a supply train leaving the next morning.

The supply train was taking the miscellaneous weapons from the conscripts back to Owen-nap. Most of them would be melted down.

When they left, we allowed the professional army to break camp, and to their surprise, we rearmed them. I stood on a wagon and announced they were still in the army of Tintagel. The only difference was that I was the leader. My title would now be Count of Cornwall, and their pay rate just doubled. That was one way to get cheers.

Interspersing the troops was an all-day event. Once in order of march, we set out with our supply train in the rear. I tried to talk Eleanor into going home, but she wanted to see this to the end.

With scouts out, we proceeded to Tintagel. It was amazing how fast we made it. With our troops pushing them, the conscripts made good time. The closer we got to Tintagel, the more the conscripts started peeling off to their home villages.

By the time we got to Tintagel, only two hundred conscripts were left.

The city gates were closed when we arrived. I had a Sergeant ride out with a white flag, and a man came out through a postern door.

He was brought to me. I introduced myself as the Count of Cornwall from Owen-nap.

He retorted, "I don't care who you are or what you call yourself. King Geraint will have your head."

I replied, "I doubt it. I have his."

I didn't. We had buried him and his cohorts beside the road after I had them looted. No use in throwing good money away, and someone would dig them up if it was known that we hadn't looted. Heck, I would have dug them up if someone was so dumb as to bury them with their riches.

War in this day and age was total. No one would have been surprised if I had all of Geraint's troops put to death. The surprise would be that so few died.

I had two of the Senior Sergeants of Geraint's old forces brought forward, and they related to the emissary what had transpired.

He asked if one of them could accompany him back inside and relate what happened to Geraint's Head Steward, who was in charge of Tintagel Keep and town while Geraint was on campaign. I knew this was a ploy to get the Sergeant away from me so he could tell the true tale. I had no problem with that, as the tale that had been told was true.

It took three hours, but the emissary returned with the Sergeant with a question.

"Will the town be sacked?"

"There has been no resistance. Why would I sack my town?"

The emissary turned and waved his arms, and the gates were opened.

Tintagel was mine. But there now was the problem of where to settle the troops. I could have sent the Tintagel troops back to their barracks, but I didn't like the idea of them being inside the town and my forces outside. A closed gate and I would have a big problem, especially if I were inside the Keep when the gate was closed.

To satisfy my cynical nature, I had the Tintagel troops camp outside of town with eleven hundred of my men with them. Two hundred of my people would stay in the barracks.

With that decided, I went into my new Capital, the fabled home of King Arthur of Legend.

There was a multitude of events that had to occur when taking over a city or even a town of five thousand. The first was to institute patrols to keep the peace. These would be my soldiers, not trained police.

There is a difference. Soldiers are trained to break things and kill people. Police are supposed to be trained to keep the peace, prevent crime, and catch criminals.

Since the Owen-nap troops wouldn't know the city, we had one of the late King Geraint's soldiers accompany them. Fortunately, there was a current map with details available in the Keep. One of my Senior Sergeants, Thomas Boatman, had a level head on him, so I put him in charge of the Patrols. He would become our first Chief of Police.

There have been many organizations since ancient history charged with some of these functions. The first formal police force was founded by Sir Robert Peel in England in 1829. Hence the term 'Bobbies'. Ours would predate that by a thousand years.

When the police force was up and running, we would spread it to every Barony and District in Cornwall. There would be local Constables.

The next step was to organize a nightsoil crew. The streets were a mess, to say the least. Later a sewage system would be put in place and running water available, but I wanted to make an immediate visual impact.

There had to be a sewage pit or cesspool outside of the city, but we needed lime to keep the stink down. Luckily there was a large lime operation, including a kiln not that far away. The kiln operator was thrilled to get our business.

Lady Agnes had accompanied us to Tintagel with a group of her young nurses. Using their MASH tent, they started to round up the street children. Forty children ranging in age from three to twelve were rounded up. They were fed, clothed, and given a bed to sleep on. It was the bath and shaved heads for lice that had them squealing.

The older orphans had been conscripted.

A local crime boss had paid off the King's men. Everyone knew who he was and that he was untouchable. I had him brought to me in chains.

When he was brought in front of me, he sputtered, "I've paid my dues."

"Were the dues the right to rule over crime in this town?"

The stupid man said, "Yes."

"Guilty through confession, hang him."

Thus, ending organized crime in our city. At least for a while. Criminals like him were the cockroaches of society. In my time, the joke was that in the event of nuclear war, only the roaches would survive. I didn't see the humor in it.

The Keep itself had been kept in good condition. This was because the Steward took his duties seriously. Even Lady Agnes was impressed with how clean he kept the place, even the kitchen. There would be no changes in the Steward, Head Cook, or their extensive staff.

Only the beggars on the street were left needing help. It being a small town, there weren't that many beggars. Only about forty of them. Some were beyond help, either truly crippled or mentally unstable. Since it was a small town, the town mayor could identify which beggars could not help themselves.

Mayor was not his real title. That was what it translated to me. The truly helpless beggars were to be taken to a farm where they would be given duties appropriate for their condition. They would be well treated.

Then there were the professional beggars. They were hale of mind and limb. They preferred begging than to try to earn a living. You could call them lazy, but they weren't. They put more effort and ingenuity into faking disabilities than any job would have asked. When you came down to it, I didn't understand what motivated them and didn't care.

I put them on a project. The port of Tintagel was hardly used because of its exposure to the Celtic Sea. There had been a breakwater to protect the harbor, but it had worn away from the constant storms that plagued the coast. The breakwater was going to be built back up. The beggars were the first workers. Any criminals caught would serve their sentence by hauling rocks.

I sentenced the beggars to one year of working on the breakwater. Afterward, they could find a job, leave the area, or find themselves back hauling rocks.

The breakwater would be a many-year project. It would end up several wagons wide with a paved road on top. For the immediate benefit of a mole, stones would bring the breakwater up to its old heights.

My reasoning was to make ship trade possible again and let the citizens see that things would improve. A few trading ships and everyone's standard of living would improve.

That took care of the immediate actions required in Tintagel. Still, there were other Barons than those in my orbit.

My best source of information proved to be the Keep's Head Steward. I'm not sure that he had a name.

I asked him, "It seems awkward to keep calling you Steward or Head Steward; what is your name?"

He replied. "It has been so long that I'm not sure I remember. I prefer Steward, if you will. Head Steward seems so presumptuous."

"How many years have you held your position?"

"If I remember correctly, fifty-seven years."

I declared, "Steward, you can be called whatever you want."

I knew people like him. He would serve until the day he died. If I retired him, he would be dead in a week. He was too good for that fate.

"I have a question: how many other Baronies are there in Cornwall, not including mine?"

"There are fifteen, My Lord. Twelve of the Barons accompanied King Geraint and suffered his fate."

"What about the other three?"

"They are on the border by Wales. They defend against incursions."

"What about the border with Wessex."

"It is open to King Ine. He defeated King Geraint and required the border to be kept open to his troops."

"Why hasn't he taken over Cornwall."

"There is nothing here that they would want. We are a poor country. Not much good farmland, no good seaport. No mines of importance."

King Ine hadn't learned about what we were doing in the Owen-naps area. If I didn't get that border under control, he would march in and take it all.

"So, you are telling me that a dozen Keeps are out there with no leadership?"

"Not at all, My Lord, each Baron would have left someone in charge while he was gone."

This was an urgent problem.

I called my council together. It now consisted of Eleanor, Lewanniet, Bolventor, and my three Senior Sergeants.

After hours of discussion, it was decided that Barons Lewanniet and Bolventor would visit each Keep and assure those in charge that they would remain in charge for the foreseeable future. Each would visit six Keeps and take one hundred twenty men with them.

They would leave twenty men at each Keep supporting whoever was in charge. I made the decision that no woman would go on this trip. Not that I didn't think they could do the job, but the attitudes that are prevalent in this day and age would make it difficult.

When I asked several women soldiers if this was a problem, they told me they weren't stupid. Good to know.

If there were a young son or daughter to inherit, they would do so. I didn't want to face a civil war in the future. Of course, there was the point that I had killed their Baron, and they might resent that. I would worry about that later. The two Barons would report on how the incumbents reacted.

We all sighed in relief when Joan Bolventor announced she was pregnant and marrying Baron Pensilva. Eleanor both hoped they remained in lust until they could learn to love.

I don't think her dad was happy, but what son-in-law is ever good enough for Daddy's girl?

I chose to go to the three Baronies on the Welch Marches. They didn't call them that, but I remembered how the English had the March Lords to fend off Welsh raiders.

All received me warmly until I told them what I had to offer and would require of them. I offered no taxes for five years. Our crossbows and bolts with training support. All I asked of them was they continue to keep the Welsh at bay.

Considering they were fellow Britons, they weren't friendly at all. I'm afraid I will have to conquer them, which will be a pain as their Keeps are on high hills.

In the meantime, the Barons took everything I was telling them with a grain of salt. They would wait and see what I came through with.

When I got back to Tintagel, there was a distraught Eleanor waiting for me. She had just got word her father had died. Nothing on how he died, just that he died.

The message from his wife Catherine told us that his body was being held on ice until Eleanor could come home.

Within hours, we were on the grueling week-long journey home. Accompanied by ten guards and spare horses, we rode from first light until dark. We were exhausted when we arrived in Owen-nap. We had to spend a day resting before we could ride to Saltash.

Word had been sent from Owen-nap that we were on our way to arrange the funeral in two days.

At Saltash, at last, we went directly to the Keep. Eleanor and Catherine, the late Baron's second wife, hugged each other and cried. Later, Catherine described his death, which she witnessed. It was at dinner, and suddenly, he clutched his chest and dropped dead. A classic massive heart attack.

The funeral was in the Saltash Church, full of standing room only. The streets were lined while we escorted his body back to the Keep to be interred with his first wife. His people truly loved him.

Catherine had arranged the wake while waiting for us to arrive. It was held in the Keep's courtyard with tables laden with food and ale by the barrel. After dark, a huge bonfire was lit. The Baron always loved a good party.

Eleanor and I sat down with Catherine the next day and assured her she could live in the Keep with her maids as long as she lived or chose to go elsewhere. We would bear all the expenses. The Baron loved her and would have wanted her taken care of.

There were no children from their marriage, so there would be no succession issues. Even though he had surrendered his title to me, if there were children, there could be problems.

We had to head back to Tintagel after the funeral, but we spent several days in Owen-nap taking care of administrative business.

We checked on Frank Goldman's wife and children to ensure they were doing okay. They were, but Miriam was worried about Frank's safety on his trip. There was nothing I could say to that. It was dangerous.

I took the time to check on our various developmental operations. Tom Smith was getting richer by the day. His ironworks crew turned out crossbows by the dozens and bolts by the hundreds.

Peter Owen-nap had separated phosphorus and safely stored it in a cave he had dug out for safety. I told him we might need it in the not-too-distant future, so add to his stockpile as he could.

The big surprise was Jude Glassman. He had come up with a workable black powder mix. It was blasting quality, not good for cannons, but we were on the way. I told him to keep at it. We could use all the powder he could make and keep trying to refine it.

I had taken Cornwall.

Now the question was, could I keep it?

The End of Book 2

Back Matter

Go to my website to find out more about my books and why I am a modern-day pirate.

enelsonauthor.com

Be on the lookout for Book 3: Count coming soon.

Printed in Great Britain
by Amazon

31316797R00178